City of Orgies

City of orgies, walks and joys,

City whom that I have lived and sung in your midst will one day make you illustrious,

Not the pageants of you, not your shifting tableaus, your spectacles, repay me,

Not the interminable rows of your houses, nor the ships at the wharves,

Nor the processions in the streets, nor the bright windows, with goods in them,

Nor to converse with learn'd persons, or bear my share in the soiree or feast;

Not those, but as I pass O Manhattan, your frequent and swift flash of eyes offering me love,

Offering response to my own – these repay me,

Lovers, continual lovers, only repay me.

Walt Whitman, *Leaves of Grass* (1891–92)

D1545990

SEX IN THE CITY

AN ILLUSTRATED HISTORY

ALISON MADDEX

FOREWORD BY CAMILLE PAGLIA

UNIVERSE

First published in the United States of America in 2002

by UNIVERSE PUBLISHING

A Division of Rizzoli

International Publications, Inc.

300 Park Avenue South

New York, NY 10010

02   03   04   05   06   /   10   9   8   7   6   5   4   3   2   1

Produced by Archetype Press, Inc.

Project Director: Diane Maddex

Designer: Robert L. Wiser

Printed in South Korea

Library of Congress Card Number: 2002110524

ISBN 0-7893-0808-8

Page 2: A real New York welcome.

Pages 12–13: 1850 letter describing a court case related to erotic drawings.

Pages 88–89: Gay men sunbathing on the Hudson River piers in the 1970s.

Pages 156–57: *Parades and Changes* (1965) by the Anna Halprin Dance Company.

Page 336: Donna Britt at the Statue of Liberty.

CONTENTS

Th* here are many cities of sin — Paris, Berlin, New Orleans, San Francisco, Hollywood, Las Vegas. But only New York, with its aggressive commercialism and monumental architecture, truly resembles the most notorious of them all — Babylon. Abandoned in ruins more than two thousand years ago, Babylon lingers in cultural memory because Judeo-Christianity formed its strict moral and sexual system in opposition to that pagan capital.

Urbanization virtually always means sexual liberalization. Ancient literature pitted virtuous countryside against dissolute city, where lambs go astray. Pastoral and agrarian life is slow and conservative: clan and tribe enforce tradition and curb individualism. Cities, however, are shifting ground where people reinvent themselves. Trade is dynamic, widening perspective and bringing cultural influences from abroad. Identity and status in cities are signaled by highly stimulating visual cues. New communities coalesce, often defined by sexual activity, a release from urban tensions as well as a consolation for absent affection. Anonymity and transience spur sex, which is why ports of call are known for their menu of short-order pleasures. Through competition and efficiency, city sex automatically becomes an industry, meeting impulse with instant gratification.

Like New York, the financial center of the world, Babylon was the most important commercial city of its era. Its position in southern Mesopotamia (modern Iraq) at the crossroads of trade routes from India to Egypt and Anatolia brought it immense wealth and power along with a reputation for sexual licentiousness. Old Testament prophets prayed for the destruction of Babylon, reviled just as New York is now as a decadent symbol of the secular West for Muslim fundamentalists. The impious tower of Babel in

Genesis was the great ziggurat (stepped tower) of Babylon that tourists in antiquity flocked to see (Gen. 11:4). Mesopotamia's ziggurats, sacred mountains tapping divine energy, were the ancestors of Manhattan's electrifying skyscrapers, the proud towers against which America's enemies conspire. The Hebrews saw Babylon up close during their fifty-year Babylonian Captivity, when thousands were deported to serve King Nebuchadnezzar after he burned Jerusalem in 586 B.C. The Hebrews were repulsed by the idolatry and hedonism of Babylonian life, with its dancers, prostitutes, perfumed, long-haired men, and sodomites. The prophets savor Babylon's fate: "Babylon is fallen, is fallen," rejoices Isaiah (Isa. 21:9).

In the New Testament's Book of Revelation, Babylon is fused with imperial Rome. St. John sees the city as a whore clothed in purple and scarlet and bedecked with gold, jewels, and pearls. She rides a scarlet, seven-headed, horned beast and holds a golden cup "full of abominations and filthiness of her fornication," which intoxicate the world. On her forehead are the words, "BABYLON THE GREAT, THE MOTHER OF HARLOTS" (Rev. 17:4–5). This is Ishtar, the Mesopotamian mother goddess representing love and fertility as well as war and death. She was the planet Venus and the lion tamer who descended in sexual obsession to the underworld. Her festivals were public orgies of sex and mob drunkenness. Many of her priests were eunuchs who had castrated themselves in her honor. In ceremonies for Babylon's chief god, the biblical Ba'al, a virgin climbed to the top of the ziggurat, where the god had intercourse with her on a golden bed.

Despite its churches and synagogues, New York City is a pagan metropolis, and Venus is its star. Like Babylon, Manhattan nestles between two rivers and is laid out in streets at right angles, a geometry that cages and intensifies its animal energies and spills them to the margins (the wharves, Greenwich Village, etc.). New York's stone canyons and penthouse arbors recall Babylon's high walls and hanging gardens, hailed by the ancients among the Seven Wonders of the World and mythically identified with the Garden of Eden. Atop Babylon's outer wall ran a spectacular, eleven-mile causeway, the world's first elevated highway, prefiguring New York's. For mortar, Babylonian architects used what the Bible calls "slime": bitumen from natural wells of asphalt, New York's modern paving (Gen. 11:3). Babylon's mud-brick walls were faced with public art, gleaming, colored enameled tiles with bas-reliefs of savage beasts. To the south of the city was a colossus (like our Greek-garbed Lady Liberty), a solid-gold statue of Nebuchadnezzar that blazed in the sun. During the rites of Ishtar, scented torches lit up the night streets — an effect fully replicated only by New York, the city that never sleeps.

Like Babylon, New York is a stratified city of sharp economic contrasts. Celebrity is its idol. Fed by nonstop caravans through tunnels and bridges, it is a cornucopia of treasures and delicacies. New York is a Belshazzar's feast of sensual indulgence. Nebuchadnezzar's son, King Belshazzar, saw handwriting on the wall read by the exile Daniel as an omen of Babylon's fall: that night, the kingdom was invaded by Persia and never recovered (Dan. 5:5). Two centuries later, Alexander the Great wanted to restore Babylon and make it the capital of his empire. But the beautiful, charismatic young Greek died of a mysterious fever at Babylon, and the city was left to the desert. It was the New Jerusalem, St. Augustine's City of God, that would thrive and bequeath its sexually repressive code to Western culture. But Babylon would rise again in rebel New York, where the scarlet beast of pagan sex roams and plays in a mineral landscape of stone and tar.

— *Camille Paglia*

This book originated in the twelve exhibitions I produced from 1991 on as a gallery owner in Washington, D.C., and as an independent arts curator in Washington and New York. My constant theme was the intersection of sex, art, and culture: I have always been fascinated by basic human instincts. My ultimate ambition was to mount an exhibition of the history of sex in America, but the task proved too daunting in terms of time and budgetary constraints. I thus turned to the history of sex in America's sexiest city, New York, where I have lived and worked. Sex in New York is inextricably intertwined with art and entertainment, business and politics, and science and medicine. In this book, I have tried to chart the varieties of sexual expression in this city, from the conventional to the most extreme.

Because my background is in visual arts (including printmaking and large-scale photomontage), this is a book of images. Its perspective and juxtapositions are influenced by my experience teaching a course I created in 1992 at Shepherd College, "The History of Sexuality in Western Art." The history of sex in New York has been well written by a number of outstanding scholars, such as Timothy Gilfoyle in *City of Eros: New York City, Prostitution, and the Commercialization of Sex, 1790–1920;* John D'Emilio and Estelle B. Freedman in *Intimate Matters: A History of Sexuality in America;* Edwin G. Burrows and Mike Wallace in *Gotham: A History of New York City to 1898;* and George Chauncey in *Gay New York: Gender, Urban Culture and the Making of the Gay Male World, 1890–1940.* Several other comprehensive works were important resources for this picture history, including *Bradley Smith's American Way of Sex: An Informal Illustrated History* and Lloyd Morris's *Incredible New York:*

High Life and Low Life from 1850 to 1950. All are highly recommended as further reading on the topic of sex in New York (see Sources).

A 350-year pictorial history of New York presented in just over three hundred pages was an ambitious task, so tough choices had to be made from an enormous wealth of material. To all of those people and places left out, I apologize. Certain material was limited, of course, such as images of early New York and of marginalized ethnic and sexual groups. Sex, it must be noted, remains a taboo subject in many quarters, with the result that some material, especially from long ago, is buried deep or is no longer extant. In a few cases, "might have looked like" images are thus used for certain undocumented early persons, places, or events. All entries relate to New York City or the boroughs or in just a few instances to New York State. In addition, where certain images of true New York personalities, such as Lillian Russell, were simply more marvelous than anything else available, they were used even though they might not have been made in New York.

More than anything else, I hope that the pictures and the information bites in this book are entertaining and amusing — and maybe just a little provocative.

I also wish to thank a number of individuals and institutions who made a difference in the development and preparation of this book. First are my partner, Camille Paglia, and my ever-supportive parents, Diane (my excellent editor) and Robert Maddex, and next are my stalwart friends who encouraged me throughout the process: Amy St. John, Tim Ries, Amelia Nickles, Theresa Luckyj, Steve Ludlum, Philip Esperdy, Katy Barrett and Andrew Langhoff, and Sharples Holden and Pasquarelli of SHoP architects.

The following institutions and researchers provided extra effort with the research and illustrations: Georgia Barnhill and Terry Tremblay of the the American Antiquarian

Society, Eileen Morales and Angela Mattia of the Museum of the City of New York, Marybeth Kavanaugh of the New-York Historical Society, Nicole Simpson of the New York Public Library, Jeremy Magraw and Phil Karg of the New York Public Library's Performing Arts Library, Jim Huffman of the New York Public Library's Schomberg Center, Rosemary Cullen and Jean Rainwater of the Brown University Library, Diane Wendt and Kay Peterson of the Smithsonian Institution, Mara Vivat of the Bradley Smith Archives, Carol Greunke of the Max Waldman Archives, Donna Mussenden VanDerZee of the James VanDerZee Archives, Muna Tseng of the Tseng Kwong Chi Archives, Louise Bourgeois, the Robert Mapplethorpe Foundation, Maidenform, Inc., *Cosmopolitan, Playboy, Penthouse,* and collectors Leo Hershkowitz, Jay Gertzman, Mark Rotenberg, and George Rinhart.

For the book's vibrant design, I also thank the talented and patient Robert L. Wiser. I am additionally indebted to Alexandra Tart of Universe Publishing for her support.

And thank you to all of the participating artists and other collectors who made the stretch for me and the vibrant history of sex in New York City.

– *Alison Maddex*

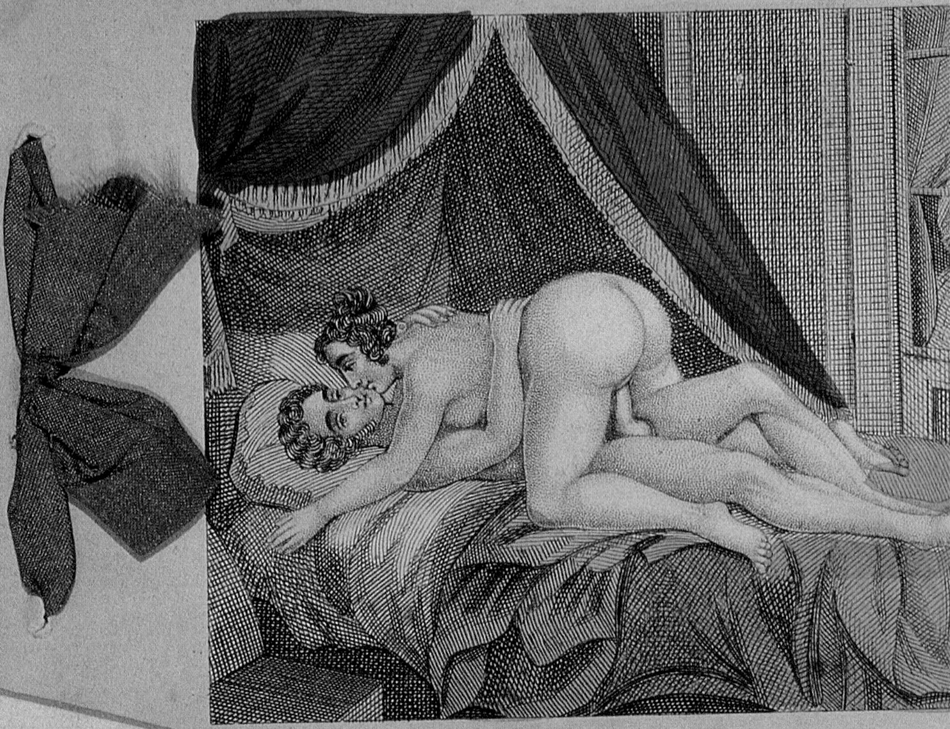

...aw Th...
here – in th...
Sale the ...
Avow indee...
at the time...
the sheets ...

his Journal

duly sworn

on the

said city,

Sweeney — now

act of offering for

merited lewd, ~~obscene~~

cent pictures they were

enclosed between

books in his posses

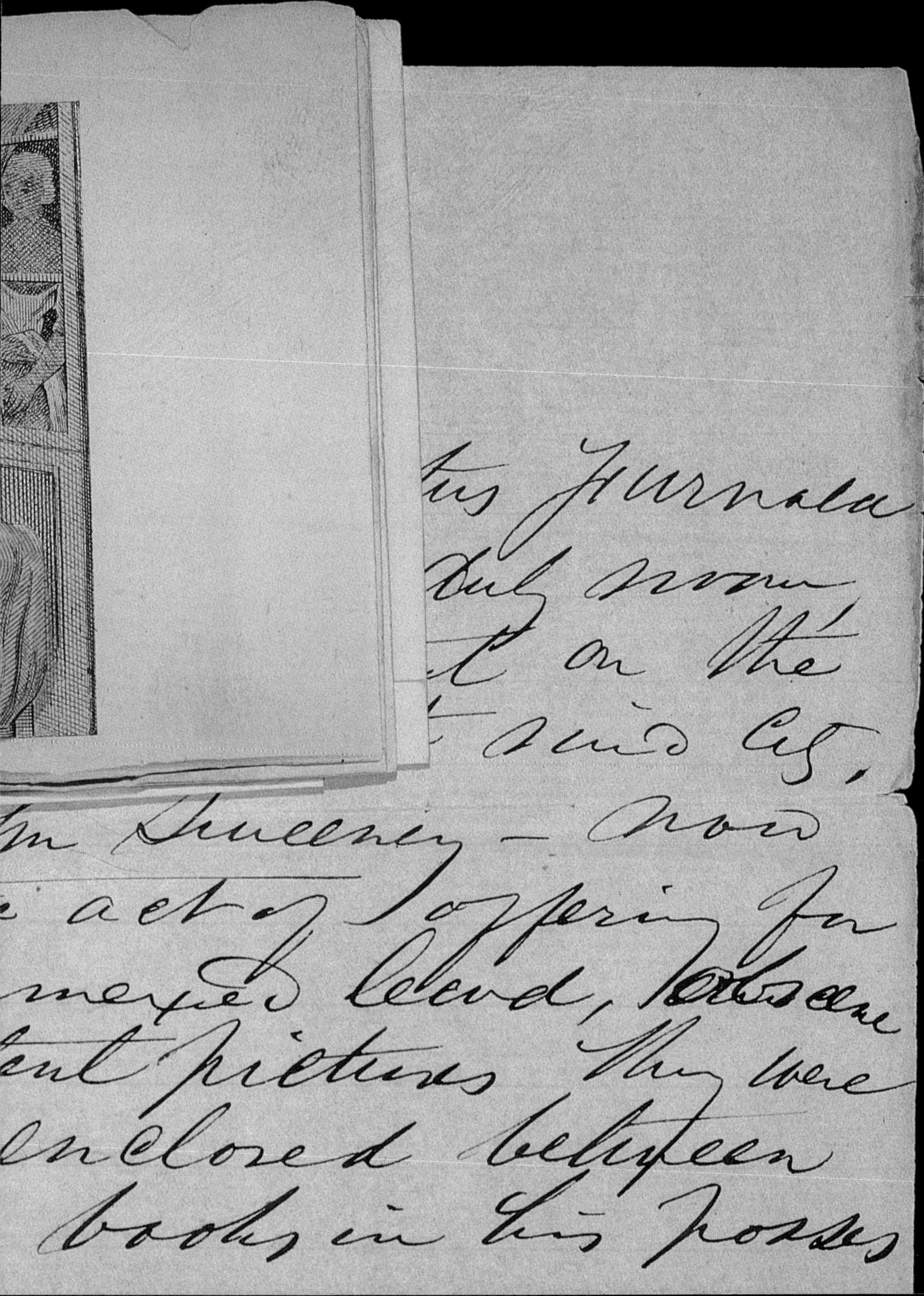

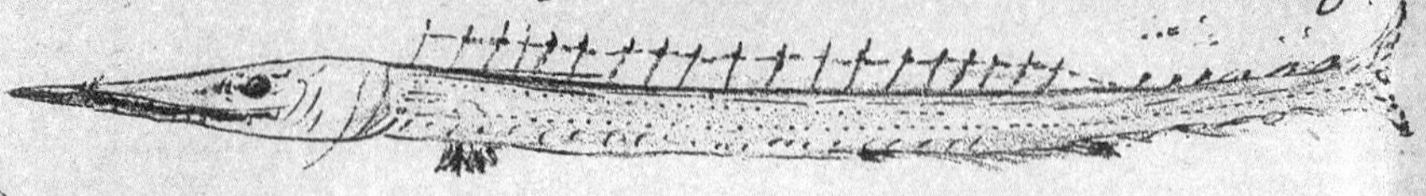

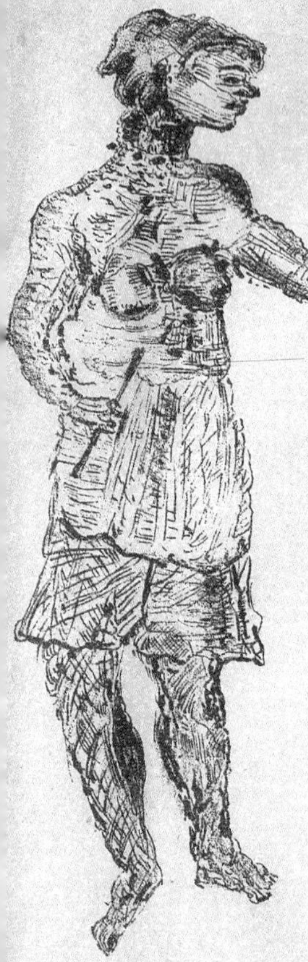

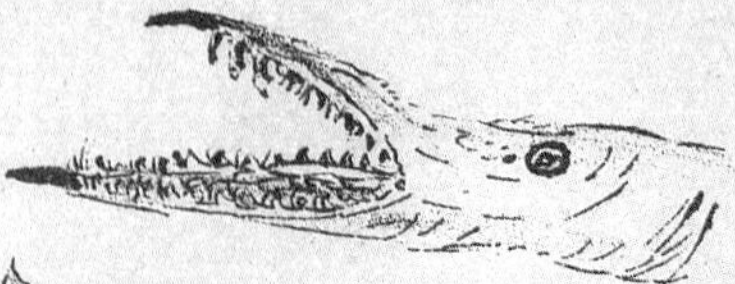

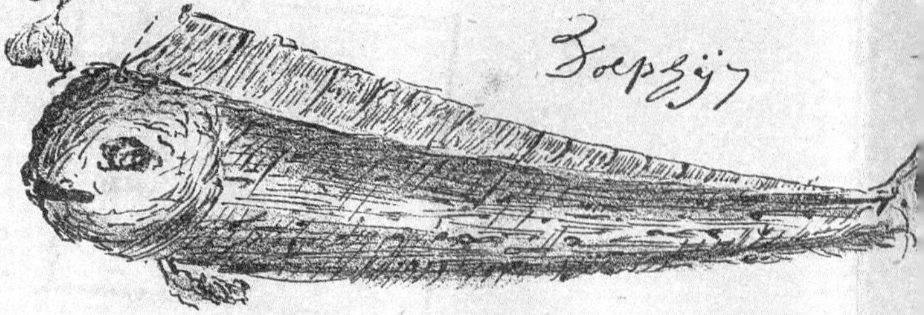

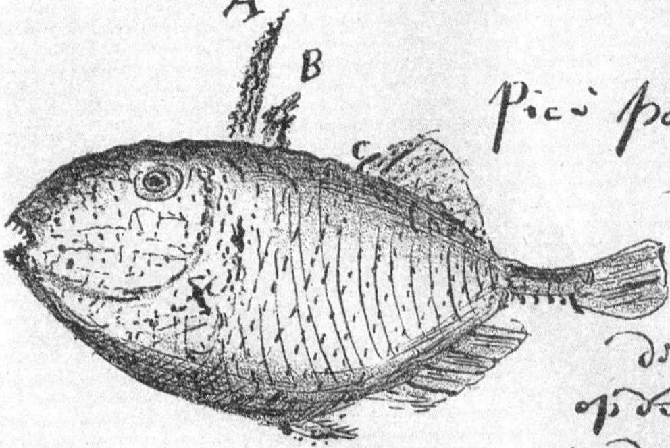

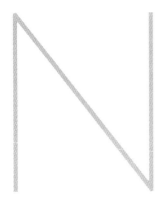

ew York has always been about the power of the individual, about expressing oneself in the most dramatic way possible. The tale of sex in the city is one of real men — and some powerful women too. Although the Delaware Indians on the lower Hudson River called themselves Lenape ("real men"), it was the local Lenape Indian women who exerted an exotic appeal for the first settlers on Manhattan: the Calvinist men of the Dutch West India Company, who founded New Amsterdam in the 1620s as a trading post of the Dutch mercantile empire. Amerindian women who had sex with European men became part of the fur trade and were consequently known as trade girls. Around 1638 a sergeant in the company troops was punished for illegal trading and sleeping with a Lenape woman. To the Europeans, this was considered prostitution, a pursuit that supposedly gave its name to a small fort the Dutch erected near the mouth of the Delaware Bay, which was known as the Whorekil (variously Hoerenkil, Horekill, and Hoorekill). The Lenape are thought to have become outraged that so many of their offspring had Dutch blood, one result of the settlers' desire to perpetuate economic and political ties with the natives. Director-General Willem Kieft strictly enforced the 1638 ban on Dutch-Indian relations. Back home in the Netherlands, unmarried Dutch women were known for their public kissing, lewd talk, and general lack of regard for chastity. With not too many of them around, what was a guy to do? ♥

Doxies with Moxy

The Dutch Calvinists in New Amsterdam had strict sexual customs, but the treatment of women under Roman-Dutch law, as in Holland, was liberal by today's standards. A strong woman meant a strong household. Prenuptial agreements put a wife's rights in writing — she could own property before and after marriage, conduct business, and hold onto common property at her husband's death. Yet a wife was never her husband's equal. In New Amsterdam, as in Amsterdam, "bawds" and "doxies" also abounded. Grietjen Reyniers, considered by some to be New York's first madam, allegedly found a broomstick handy for taking the measure of the male members of sailors visiting her home, probably located near the waterfront. Griet and her husband were expelled from New Amsterdam in 1639, after which they went to Long Island to start a farm. Another wench, Nanne Beeche, caused quite a stir at a party at Claes Cornelissen's when, in the presence of her husband, according to Edwin G. Burrows and Mike Wallace, she "fumbled at the front breeches of most of all those who were present. The crew of a departing ship saw her on the shore and began chanting 'Whore, Whore, Two pound butter's whore!'"

Aphrodisiac City

One of New York's oldest customs came in with the Dutch in the mid-seventeenth century. Two weeks before New Year's Day, young men made a list of the ladies they intended to call on — fifty or a hundred names. Out early, adorned with trinkets and ribbons, they left their calling cards and at every house they entered would call out: "Is

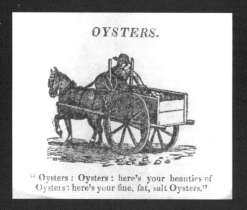

"Oysters : Oysters : here's your beauties of Oysters : here's your fine, fat, salt Oysters."

Miss at home? I am come to drink to her health and wish her a happy New Year." The men rushed madly in and out, boasting about the numbers of calls they made, and the ladies loved to total up all their cards. Every house became "liberty hall" on New Year's, with cognac and kisses all given gratis. Another elixir, that of the oyster, may contain the secret why native New Yorkers have been a bit more randy than others. New York Harbor and the surrounding bays contained an extraordinary abundance of clams, crabs, and oysters. In 1763 a primitive saloon that opened in a Broad Street cellar became the first in the country to serve oysters to the public. Tons of discarded oyster shells along the shore inspired the Dutch to dub the area Pearl Street.

Painted by J.G.Chapman.   Steel Plate.   Engraved By M.Osborne.

Old Times on Broadway.

Just Warming Up

For Dutch Protestant and French Walloon settlers in New Amsterdam, family became the central economic unit. Young people were taught to channel sexual desire toward courtship, marriage, and childbearing. Children likely observed some sexual activity in their small house and in the barnyard; bestiality, however, was not condoned. Puritan evangelicals tried to suppress lust, although courtship — unchaperoned but usually in public view — was perfect for exploring sexual desires. A suitor who traveled a long distance to visit his intended in a small, cold house could, with parental approval, spend the night in bed with her. The hitch with bundling (called *questing* in Holland) was that the couple had to remain fully clothed or keep a "bundling board" between

them. When the rules of bundling were defied and a pregnancy resulted, the couple were expected to marry. Bundling prevailed for a hundred years in the New World, but by 1756 the upper classes of New York and New England had introduced the sofa for courting. Marriages were not arranged, although parents always made the final decision. After 1664, when the English took over Manhattan, making it New York, laws similar to New England's were established. Divorce was liberalized in cases where one party was deserted. This followed the Puritan example, but New York law required a five-year waiting period.

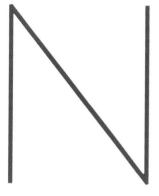ew York is a city of classes and contrasts. Its superior harbor nourished a great trading colony, providing commercial success to multitudes. Early explorers came from diverse places and circumstances, but all came hungry for riches and personal and national aggrandizement. Prosperity was blatant: in the seventeenth and eighteenth centuries New Yorkers were noted for dressing more gaily and with greater ostentation than proper Bostonians or reserved Philadelphians. As the port grew, taverns and bawdy women multiplied with it, and high spirits filled the night. The British leisure class maintained gentility by curbing vulgar behavior and discouraging crass language. Women's fashions in particular betrayed social standing: dress was governed by strict rules of etiquette. Fifth Avenoodles promenading uptown with the tide of fashion in the mid-1700s showed the world that America was no longer an untamed place. Man conquered nature, but man conquered man along the way. Manhattan was built on the backs of the lower classes, including women on their backs. As the rich got richer and more entrenched, the toiling working class and other free spirits looked for every crack in the stony cityscape to let human nature loose from earthly laws, expectations, and inhibitions — anywhere, anytime. A woman alighting from a trolley about 1848 is caught between the Third Avenue world of the "respectable poor" and New York's gentility. In this "go ahead" age, women's petticoated skirts allowed for little mobility — this one is stiffened with wholesale coffee-bag burlap. The bored conductor figures she's a good "grind." Sexual expression, hidden and covert, continues to be New York's wildest weed. ♥

Volksvermaken

Newly immigrated New Netherlanders celebrated *Volksvermaken* (folk pleasures) in the mid-1660s (forty percent of the population was Dutch, the rest being German, English, native, and black). The Dutch tradition of commencing Shrove (Fat) Tuesday with a bacchanal of food and drink continued in New Amsterdam, with young men parading through the streets in drag. May Day was welcomed with a dance around the maypole, an emblem of fertility (*May* comes from a Norse word meaning to shoot out new growth). For the working class, the place to be for a little gambling, drinking, and game playing was a tavern, grog shop, or pot house selling pots of intoxicants; both women and men smoked pipes in these places. In 1654 Director-General Peter Stuyvesant (d. 1672) banned the pagan rites and ordered the doors of brewers and innkeepers closed at 9 P.M. The Dutch upper classes, who had once joined in, had become more genteel.

Sexual Commerce on the Battery

Around 1744 one of the country's earliest travel writers, Dr. Alexander Hamilton, remarked that an after-dusk stroll on the Battery "was a good way for a stranger to fit himself with a courtesan; for that place was the general rendezvous of the fair sex of that profession after sunset." With more troops and privateers and more money coming into the city, normally low-profile prostitutes turned to more aggressive marketing tactics. Some went as far as greeting prospective clients aboard anchored ships. Sexual activity and commerce, including a great deal of homosexual behavior, continued on the Battery over the years.

Lordy!

The early eighteenth-century governor of New York, Edward Hyde, Lord Cornbury, supposedly liked to dress in his wife's clothes and parade around his British fort. The story goes that he was mistaken for a prostitute one night on Broadway and was hauled to the stockade. Lord Cornbury was also said to have had an ear fetish, giving the green light for visitors to official state functions to fondle his wife's ears. Patricia Bonomi, emerita professor at New York University, doesn't believe a word of it. The undated portrait entitled *Unidentified Woman, formerly Edward Hyde, Lord (Viscount) Cornbury* by an unidentified artist, she suggests, could be of anyone: Cornbury would never have chosen to be depicted this way because cross-dressing was then considered an abomination. If meant as a satire, a quick sketch or an engraving might have been done, rather than an expensive oil painting. Other than a memoir by a seventy-six-year-old woman, the only evidence that the governor was a transvestite comes from four letters, probably written by enemies who were miffed at the high-handed way he took charge of the city. Lord Cornbury nonetheless was indeed a troublemaker. He was a deadbeat, and even his wife was known to nick other aristocratic ladies' clothes. In 1708 he was thrown into debtors' prison, after which he returned to England to assume his father's estate and a new title: the third earl of Clarendon. His legacy lives on in the name of Hyde Park, New York.

A Woman of Pleasure

In New York's early days most, if not all, erotica came from Europe. One novel that enjoyed enormous popularity in the States was *Memoirs of a Woman of Pleasure* (1749), by John Cleland. Later known as *Fanny Hill,* it was and still is a sophisticated piece of pornographic literature, centered around the activities of a London prostitute. *Fanny Hill* acquired a bad name for itself in part because of the illustrations that could be found in later underground editions, like this one from 1776. "Rumor has it that Cleland may have written *Memoirs* to prove that he could produce a book about sex without including an offending word," suggests Marianna Beck, a sex educator. "Thus, in circumventing colloquial terms like 'cunt' and 'prick,' Cleland came up with wonderful euphemisms: over fifty metaphors for penis, such as 'master member of the revels,' 'instrument of pleasure,' 'picklock,' and, oddly, 'nipple of love.' For vagina, he invented 'soft laboratory of love,' 'pleasure-thirsty channel,' 'embowered bottom cavity,' and 'abyss of joy.'" In 1821, in the first known obscenity case in the United States, *Fanny Hill* was banned in Massachusetts. When Grove Press openly published the book in 1963, it was attacked by "decency" groups. The highest courts of New Jersey and Massachusetts declared it obscene, yet on March 21, 1966, the U.S. Supreme Court cleared *Memoirs of a Woman of Pleasure* for wider enjoyment.

Holy Ground

The Revolutionary War (1775–83) kept the taverns and brothels humming in New York. Lieutenant Isaac Bangs, worried that his troops would catch "the Fatal Disorder," visited the "Holy Ground," a notorious prostitution district that ran two blocks along Church, Vesey, and Barclay Streets from 1770 through the early nineteenth century; the city's most expensive whorehouses were on land owned by the Episcopal Church. Bangs saw many prostitutes, branding them "brutal creatures." During the British occupation of the city from 1776 to 1783, "hags," "strums," and "jills" could also be found at the foot of Broad Street in Canvas Town, named for the roofs that replaced those lost in the fire of 1776.

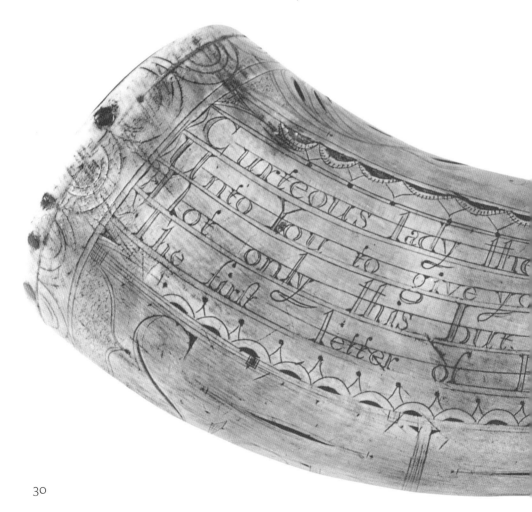

City-wide whorehouse riots broke out in 1793 after Harry Bedlow ("Lawyer Smith") was acquitted of raping a sailor's daughter, the seventeen-year-old seamstress Lanah Sawyer. The two had "walked out" on a number of occasions, and in eighteenth-century Manhattan it was widely assumed that when a working girl walked out with a gentleman, sex was on the evening's agenda. But the public saw this seduction of an innocent girl as a symbol of ambiguous social rules governing the encounters of strangers on big city streets. A lonely guy might have kept company with this powder horn from Crown Point, New York, made in 1761 and owned by Stephen Tambling. Inscriptions and art are attributed to a Lake George artist — the first letters of each line spell out CUNT.

War and Sex

During the Revolutionary War both sides
had women camp followers who acted as
nurses and sexual partners and also
smuggled rum and provisions. The
wealthier British had more, and many
sympathizers joined the redcoats along the
way. British men were smitten with
American girls, but rapes caused many
neutrals to turn American patriots. The
Baroness von Riedesel, the wife of a
Hessian general, made detailed accounts of
her travels, describing the amorous affairs
of her friends. General William Howe, she
noted, was "singing, drinking and amusing
himself with the wife of a commissary —
who was his mistress." The baroness gave
regular parties "to gain the affection of the
inhabitants and provide innocent pleasures
for the officers, and thus keep them from
visiting public houses and bad company."

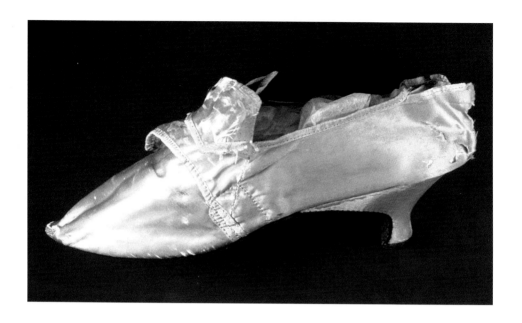

Sophisticated Sex

A fashionable shoe would have been part of a smart ensemble worn by refined New Yorkers. This ivory satin example with a pointed toe and tongue and a high, slim heel was worn by First Lady Martha Washington about 1785–90 and inherited by Alexander Hamilton's wife, Elizabeth. To distinguish themselves from the vulgar masses, the upper classes wore clean, fresh, stylish clothing and accessories and exhibited self-control. Bad language, lewd behavior, and wild emotions were not acceptable. Genteel New Yorkers could prove their refinement at the yearly Governor's Ball or at weekly turtle feasts, where they might dance formal dances, recite literature, and speak foreign languages — always with perfect diction and posture. Young men and women could mingle with their own kind on chaperoned "routs" and "frolics." Refined bachelors knew to keep sexual activity confined to serving girls and prostitutes. Single ladies knew better than to have any fun at all.

The Federalist

An illegitimate child born in Nevis, British West Indies, Alexander Hamilton (1757–1804) arrived in New York City in 1772, when he was about fifteen. He wed Elizabeth Schuyler, whose family was rich and powerful. After he became the nation's first secretary of the treasury in 1789, he was visited one day by Maria (Mrs. James) Reynolds, who asked him for money so she could leave her abusive husband. Hamilton decided to help her in more ways than one, and a relationship ensued. James Reynolds, a convicted swindler, ignored the liaison, choosing instead to blackmail Hamilton for a position in the Treasury Department. Although he paid the couple some money, Hamilton refused to appoint Reynolds, who then falsely accused Hamilton of giving him money from the treasury to speculate in the stock market. Hamilton went to Secretary of State Thomas Jefferson, admitted the affair, and explained that the payoff came from his own money. Because he refused to barter American honor for his own, Hamilton retained the confidence of peers such as George Washington. But Hamilton lost his final battle with honor when he died in 1804 at the hands of his political rival, Aaron Burr, in a duel across the river in Weehawken, New Jersey.

ARISTOTLE's
COMPLEAT
MASTER-PIECE.

In Three Parts:

Displaying the Secrets of Nature in the Generation of Man.

Regularly digefted into Chapters and Sections, rendering it far more ufeful and eafy than any yet extant.

To which is added,

A Treafure of **HEALTH**;

OR, THE

FAMILY PHYSICIAN;

Being Choice and Approved Remedies for all the feveral Diftempers incident to Human Bodies.

The Twenty-Sixth Edition.

Printed and Sold by the Bookfellers, 1755.

The Original Joy of Sex

Usually sold under the counter, the sex manual *Aristotle's Compleat Masterpiece* (1755) was extremely popular throughout America. A combination of folklore and scientific guesswork first published in London seventy years earlier, the book presented sex as natural and healthy — promoting the English belief that pleasure in sex was necessary for conception. Reproduction continued to be the primary goal of sex, however; no contraception information was provided. The mysterious "Aristotle" cautioned that early withdrawal be avoided, lest the "fruits of the labor" be lost. Men and women were also warned to think pleasant thoughts during intercourse, and to ensure this a section entitled "Of Monstrous Births" was included.

Temptations at Home and Abroad

With its elegantly engraved romp through what seemed a more sexually liberated Europe, *A Sentimental Journey through France and Italy* (1795) would have been of great interest to post-Revolutionary New Yorkers. In his tour of America around this time, which included stops in New York and Pennsylvania, the distinguished French writer Moreau de St. Mery (1750–1819) took the sexual temperature of Americans. American women, he noted in his travel journal, were hypocritical — using vulgar language but avoiding the facts of life, and some were lesbians. They did not speak of their body parts, dividing the body instead into "stomachs" (from shoulders to waist) and "ankles" (from waist to foot). A young girl was free to have suitors call upon her and to go on walks with them without any parental intrusion, St. Mery reported, but after marriage women lived only for their husbands, becoming "the one and only servant in the house."

Such were my temptations. ———

A

SENTIMENTAL JOURNEY

THROUGH

FRANCE and ITALY.

BY

Mr. *YORICK.*

Ornamented with Elegant Engravings.

NEW-YORK:

PRINTED FOR THE BOOKSELLERS,

1795.

Black and White

About 7,500 free blacks lived in New York at the turn of the nineteenth century. Gradual emancipation had begun in 1799, but although no slaves were freed outright many found a way to freedom. To justify continued economic and social subordination of blacks, English colonists had suggested that they were closer to nature and savagery and thus were more sexual and aggressive — especially when compared with their own prudish natures. Whether or not they supported slavery, most white Americans from North to South opposed interracial blending (the word *miscegenation* was coined in 1864 by Democrats Goodman Croly, managing editor of the *New York World,* and George Wakeman, a *World* reporter). Laws imposed jail time and fines for people of different races who intermixed. Yet it still happened. Racial tensions existed, even in "live and let live" New York. On December 15, 1808, Captain James Dunn was tried for assault with intent to seduce Sylvia Patterson, a black woman who was the wife of James Patterson. White men who desired black women would not admit it, alleging that it was the black women who were lustful and easy.

TRIAL

OF

CAPTAIN JAMES DUNN.

Then vain is thy sweet power
To soothe my pained breast.

Five Points

Five Points — centered on the intersection of Orange, Anthony, and Cross Streets
(now part of Chinatown) — was New York's most degraded sex district before and
during the Civil War (1861–65). America's first slum, it was built atop the collect
pond for the city's water, the stench of the pond adding to the area's decaying,
damp, rotting aroma. Full of new immigrants, many of them Irish, this dog-eat-dog
zone had gangs known as "shoulder hitters," tramps, drunks, illegal gambling, and
of course sex. The Old Brewery, built in 1792, housed some of the area's poorest

residents and had rooms upstairs for transients and prostitutes. The reporter George Foster remarked at midcentury that it was not unusual to find a mother and her two or three girls having hellish intercourse in the family's one room. Unlike the rest of antebellum America, Five Points was the scene of great racial diversity, including hotbeds of black-and-white sex. Newspapers fueled white fears of black sexual supremacy by frequently reporting on interracial goings-on. Attempts to raze or transform the area were thwarted by wealthy landlords — including John R. Livingston, brother of the founding father Robert Livingston — and other local entrepreneurs.

Bowery B'hoys and G'hals

Working-class men bored with dull, repetitive work that would probably not get them up the first rung of the social ladder looked for ways to assert themselves in public. Many frequented the crude entertainment of the Bowery, which ran north from Chatham Square to East Fourth Street, and some joined gangs, such as the Bowery B'hoys. "B'hoys" was a general handle for rowdy guys of no specific nationality who lived in predominantly male wards and frequented the Bowery theaters, dance halls, and brothels. They swaggered about downtown, parodying the Broadway cultural elite, dressed like "fancy-Dans" with stovepipe hats, red shirts, black silk ties, and flared pants and were never without the requisite stogie. Mose, the hero of Benjamin Baker's play *Glance at New York* (1848) (later *New York as It Is*) was the quintessential benevolent tough guy. A butcher and a dedicated volunteer firefighter with great strength and stamina, he loved a good fight. Mose was a symbol of masculinity — a trait of little importance to the upper class. Bowery G'hals, like Mose's girlfriend Lize, dressed garishly and wore decorative bonnets balanced on their heads. Although their b'hoys protected them, those same neighborhood gangs were known for their riotous rages against prostitutes and madams.

In the Mood Yet?

Cramped tenements, like those on the Lower East Side — once one of the world's most densely populated urban areas — were not the place for romance. In 1905, when John Sloan made this print, New York had at least 43,000 tenements, housing more than 1.5 million persons. A family might live in the kitchen and rent out the other rooms. Pungent odors abounded from the myriad culinary traditions cooking in the melting pot. Bathtubs were scarce, mattresses foul, lice and vermin proliferated, and deadly diseases were passed around. Harsh weather conditions, especially the heat of summer, exacerbated the problems. As in colonial days, when living space was tight, children got an early sex education. Still, wooing and sex, no matter what the conditions, were one escape from reality.

SEPARATE SPHERES

After the Revolution, women who had made great contributions to the cause found themselves relegated to second-class citizenship. A woman's chief duty was to stay at home and raise strong sons for the service of the republic. By the mid-nineteenth century the division of male and female realms was at its most pronounced. Men reigned over the exclusive downtown sphere of business and politics, spending their time together politicking, carousing, whoring, and rioting. This was a time of male bonding so intense that homosexual activity was not unusual. Even the poet Walt Whitman (1819–92) was known to get close to hunky workmen. The "sporting male" (confirmed bachelor) arrived on the urban scene around the 1830s. These sexual prowlers, either single or married, were of two distinct types. The "fancy men for the upper ten thousand," or "upper-tendom" b'hoys, were relatively well educated and bred, always fashionably dressed, socially aspiring, and more interested in leisure activities such as communal drinking than work. Without family nearby, the entertainments on Broadway and in saloons, the boxing ring, and gambling dens were like home. The "fancy men of the lower million" were the rough-and-tumble downtown Bowery B'hoys. Sporting men ignored conventional sexual proprieties by celebrating prostitution and justifying brothels as a way to protect their sisters and wives. (Contemporary medical texts explained that women just didn't have the same sexual needs as men.) Women were forbidden in this world of men; in fact, women in public were mostly resented or looked down upon. Independent, money-making working girls and madams were the victims of numerous vicious brothel riots in the 1830s. The domestic realm was the place for decent women. ❤

Married or Single

Most middle-class women in New York stayed close to home but, at a time when gender relations were rigid, built strong support relationships with one another, to the point of sleeping and vacationing together. One woman who ventured out into the male literary world was Catherine Maria Sedgewick (1789–1867), the author of the first American domestic novel, *A New England Tale* (1822), as well as *Poor Rich Man* (and *Rich Poor Man*) (1836), *Live and Let Live* (1837), and *Married or Single* (1857), plus several moral guidance books. An important model for Poe, Hawthorne, Melville, and Bryant, she died a spinster in New York. For her readers who felt trapped at home, working-class women might have seemed the lucky ones — joining the labor force as seamstresses and servants. When bourgeois women did venture out, they visited appropriate ladies-only places and went through ladies-only aisles in banks and post offices.

Desperately Seeking Funny Business

The first personal advertisement is thought to have run in New York around 1820. Fifteen years later James Gordon Bennet began the New York Herald *as a news-filled penny daily to capitalize on the earning potential of these "public services." His personal ads catered to bachelors and the likes of prostitutes, brothel recruiters, abortionists, black-mailers, and burglars. The upstanding public was outraged.*

Eng'd by Forrest, from a Sketch by Fredrika Bremer

T. B.
1851.

Off-Stage Tragedies

New Yorkers usually cooled to hot stage stars at any sign of immoral behavior, but this wasn't quite true in the case of the famous actor Edwin Forrest (1806–72). Known for his tragic roles as Macbeth, Hamlet, Othello, and Lear, his most memorable drama was played off-stage. In his early Bowery Theater days in the 1820s, Forrest was a downtown hero — an icon to the Bowery B'hoys and their rivals, the Dead Rabbits gang. In 1848 a feud began between him and the English actor William Charles Macready; the two rival gangs angrily headed uptown to send Macready packing. A riot ensued, causing the deaths of twenty-two persons and numerous injuries. But that scandal wasn't enough. To divorce his wife, Catherine Norton Sinclair Forrest (they were married from 1851 to 1869), Forrest accused her of infidelity. She filed a countersuit, represented by their mutual friend Nathaniel P. Willis. In *The Home Journal*, Willis charged that Forrest was not only jealous of his wife's intellect but was also trying to duck alimony payments. Naturally Forrest fired back with a libel suit and even horsewhipped Willis in Washington Square. Just before he played an engagement at the Broadway Theater, his wife won the first suit. Forrest continued to attract audiences that came to see him openly castigate his wife and Willis after each performance. It wasn't the last time scandal packed a Broadway theater.

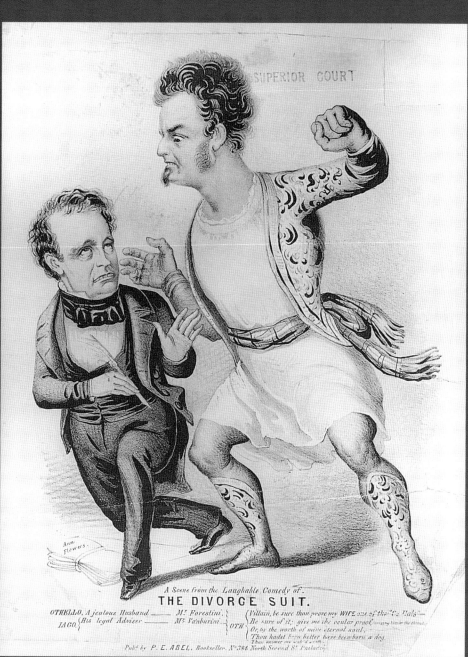

A Scene from the Laughable Comedy of

THE DIVORCE SUIT.

OTHELLO, A jealous Husband ———— M.ʳ Forestini.
IAGO, (His legal Adviser ———— M.ʳ Vanburini.

OTH (Villain, be sure thou prove my WIFE one of the "C. Hals."
Be sure of it; give me the ocular proof,
Or, by the worth of mine eternal soul.
Thou hadst been better have been born a dog.
Than answer my wak'd wrath.

Pub.ᵈ by P. E. ABEL, Bookseller, N.º 384 North Second S.ᵗ Parlaties.

Splitsville

The nineteenth century was a time of transition within the realm of the family. Although older patterns of reproduction-centered unions still lingered in rural areas and the agricultural South, New Yorkers began getting used to the new functions of families that accompanied industrialization. Couples were controlling fertility more and more, making sex not synonymous with reproduction and thereby making room for passion and love. Rather than a product of practical arrangements made by relatives, marriage grew out of courtship and dating.

Yet gender spheres

POPPING THE QUESTION.

A LOVE-LETTER.

TH

SEVE

MAT

1. One look at beauty
   Has placed a lover
2. She reads - she smil
   Is now transfixed
3. He raves – he swea
   The fowler snares th
4. The fatal knot has tied them fast,
   Oh, happiness too sweet to last!
5. The baby dear delights its Ma!
   Because it looks just like its Pa!

QUIZZING.

remained separate, with men heading out of the home to make a living (and to do a lot of other things they pleased), while women played domestic goddesses, even with dwindling families. Holding the family together was no longer an absolute necessity, but with little money and no rights for women, divorce would have been a tough decision for any wife. Nonetheless, as Currier and Ives documented, divorce was definitely on the rise.

AGE.

THE BABY.

TACES

MONY.

THE QUARREL.

BILL of COST.

Annuity.

THE DIVORCE.

ATTORNEY AT LAW.

s that
s hat .
fluttering heart
d's dart .
plights her word;
ird !
    6. But now the leaves desert the rose
      And ragged thorns themselvs diselose .
    7. She sues her lord - she's bound to win,
      She leaves his house, but keeps his tin!

Always Something to Crow About

New York State abolished slavery in 1827, but it would be almost one hundred years before a black-and-white couple wouldn't raise an eyebrow on the street. Even someone as respected as Frederick Douglass (1817–95), the freed slave and antislavery spokesman, got a razzing by the New York press. Douglass had come to New York after fleeing Baltimore in 1838, marrying his first wife, Anna Murray, here. To the outrage of whites and the dismay of blacks, in 1884 Douglass married again after Anna died, to Helen Pitts, his secretary, a feminist and a graduate of Mount Holyoke Seminary. For Douglass, his first marriage honored his mother, who was black, while his second honored his father, who was white. Why the uproar, he wondered, when he was only a few skin shades away from that of his new wife, but he could have married someone shades darker than he and given no offense.

Stiff Competition

As the twentieth century dawned, fashions loosened — women's "rainy-daisy" skirts showed a half foot of leg, and men tossed out their frock coats and boiled shirts. The Gibson Girl, created by Charles Dana Gibson (1867–1944) and modeled after his wife, Irene, might have been the first "It" girl — beautiful, elegant, and self-confident. Her aloofness drove the guys wild. With her whimsical pompadour and starched high-collar shirtwaist, she set the style of the era. The corset, as Bloomingdale's knew, remained an essential fashion statement. It put the sexual spotlight on the waist, with the bust and hips running a close second and third. Trying to make one's waist size equal to one's age at marriage may have caused impaired breathing and circulation and other deformities of the rib cage and spine, but women just wouldn't give up their symbol of virtue and refinement, even if doctors warned against corsets and their dangers to fertility. Women themselves advocated the ultrastiff contraption to establish a pecking order within their own sex.

The "Elvira" Corset.

The "ELVIRA" is what nine-tenths of the women want — a perfect though moderate-priced Corset. The result of years of close study and patient experimenting, it is conceded to-day to be the most satisfactory Corset that woman has ever worn.

It is an aid to grace, an aid to comfort, and an aid to health.

Give every other Corset its full measure of credit, and is there one among them that *combines* these three important features?

It is of very fine coutille, with extra heavy bones, 13-inch steels, high bust and back, and is the only Corset that will improve the figure without injurious or uncomfortable tight lacing. Fully guaranteed. White or drab, $3.50 and upwards. Black, $3.98 and upwards. Sold in the United States, Canada and Mexico only by

Bloomingdale Bros.,

Third Ave., cor. 59th St.,

NEW YORK,

n love and business, New York has always bred extreme behavior, but the most dramatic scandals seem to have had something to do with sex. The gruesome dispatch of Helen Jewett, a prostitute, in 1836 was quickly transformed by the penny press into the first big media sex scandal and topic of public debate on sexuality, gender, and class. In 1841 Mary Rogers, a cigar store girl, disappeared from her boarding house and was thought to have been gang raped and thrown into the Hudson River; it was later learned that an improper abortion was the cause. Edgar Allen Poe immortalized her in *The Mystery of Mary Roget* (1842). Even more chaste women such as Alice Bowlsby, a dressmaker testing her sexual freedom, met similar fates. Her body was found in a trunk at the train station in 1871, about to depart for Chicago — one of countless cases of death by botched abortions (opposite). Her doctor was found guilty of manslaughter, and her lover (seen as her seducer) committed suicide. Cures for such goings-on elicited other extremes. In the 1870s Anthony Comstock (1844–1915), the ridiculed but tolerated vice crusader extraordinaire, began campaigning to keep all sexual expression private. On the premise that lust is dangerous, he branded everything related to sex in the public sphere obscene and tried to keep any sexual literature out of circulation. In 1873 Comstock pushed through the federal Comstock Act, which outlawed the distribution of any information or object related to contraceptives. Naturally he was against abortion too. Backed by wealthy YMCA members, he established the New York Society for the Suppression of Vice to enforce existing obscenity laws and confiscated odious books. For a time, the "purity" groups and suffragists stood by him, but Comstock's intimidation tactics finally drove them away. ❤

The Innocent Boy

In April 1836, in a brothel run by Rosina
Townsend, the most desired courtesan
in the city was hacked to death with an
axe and her body set on fire. Richard
Robinson, a promiscuous clerk in the
Maiden Lane garment district, was charged
with the murder of Helen Jewett on the
basis of strong circumstantial evidence —
his blue cloak and hatchet were found in
the yard neighboring the brothel at 41
Thomas Street. Robinson may have been
trying to retrieve love letters sent to the
beautiful and intelligent Helen. The public
was divided. The lower classes slammed
the privileged "nabob" who exploited
poor young women. Reformers saw
Jewett as a young woman gone astray.
Dandies and the upper crust saw the
prostitute as a sexual temptress who
brought ruin to men and caused her own
death. Amid rumors of jury tampering,
the defendant was quickly acquitted.

Dressed to Please

Men who dressed like women were not
that unusual in the city in the late 1830s.
Rather than being seen as threats to
masculinity or as sexual predators,
effeminate transvestites were for the most
part viewed as just odd. They had sex with
"straight" males and were usually left
alone by the police. The Übermensch
"sporting press" was an exception,
describing homosexuals as "abominable
sinners," "brutal sodomites," and "beasts
who follow that unhallowed practice" and
linking homosexuality to foreigners and
the theater. Peter Sewally, a native New
Yorker also known as Mary Jones, lived in
a brothel as a housekeeper. He chose his
style of dress simply because he felt he
looked better in women's clothes and was
eventually convicted of grand larceny.
More than anything, people seemed to
be interested in his clothes.

THE MAN-MONSTER,

Peter Sewally, alias Mary Jones &c&c.

Sentenced 18th June 1836, to 5 years imprisonment at hard labor at
Sing Sing, for Grand Larceny

Published by H R Robinson, 48. Courtlandt St N.Y.

Perfect Sex

Utopian communities — Shakers, Mormons, Oneidans, free lovers, Fourierists, and others — sprang up in the early nineteenth century as variant paths on the road to spiritual perfection. All were different except for a common interest in regulating sexual impulses. Oneidans, with communes in Brooklyn and upstate New York, and the Modern Times assembly on Long Island came in for the most scrutiny by New Yorkers. The Oneida communities, including the one in Brooklyn founded by John Humphrey Noyes around 1849, practiced such lifestyles as "complex marriage," "male continence," and "mutual criticism." At Oneida everyone was married to everyone else, and women were supposedly equal to men. To cohabit, a couple had to get permission from another person or persons. Virgins were "cared for" (deflowered) by "people closest to God" (elders and central members). Menopausal women taught young men how not to ejaculate during sex, as a seed not intent on procreation was seen as a wasted seed. The group disbanded by 1879, a victim of hostility within and outside.

The Wickedest Woman in Town

She solved the problems of "ladies who had been unfortunate" and cured "diseases peculiar to females." Madame Restelle (Ann Lohman) built her successful abortion enterprise with the dollars of the elite. She was feared and despised, but her power and wealth (which bought good attorneys and a brownstone on Fifth Avenue) kept her in business. By 1840 "Madame Killer" had offices in New York, Newark, and Philadelphia; abortion was banned in 1845. Then in 1878 Anthony Comstock, the city's antivice big shot, entrapped her. A $40,000 bribe did not work. A few days after she made bail, a servant found her in the bathroom in a pool of blood: she had cut her own throat. Although New Yorkers were not sad to see her go, they severely reproached Comstock for causing her suicide.

Free Love in Every House

The free-love movement originated in the antebellum period, but Victoria Claflin Woodhull (1838–1927) shoved it into the public spotlight in the last quarter of the nineteenth century. Emphasizing love and desire over reproduction, Woodhull — a spiritualist, fortune teller, and stockbroker — maintained that sex should be consummated only with love. Marriage, she argued, was an unjust intrusion into personal life, inhibiting erotic pleasure, destroying individual happiness, and making women slaves or prostitutes.

By opposing prostitution, calling for an end to male dominance in marriage, supporting voluntary motherhood and male continence, and generally encouraging women's equality, Woodhull's theories were similar to those of "purity" reformers who wanted to clean up vice and sin. The Equal Rights Party nominated this stirring public speaker to run for president in 1872, alongside Frederick Douglass, but her free-love platform (and opposition to organized religion and possible communist leanings) failed to sweep her into office. Free lovers like Woodhull came in for the most severe criticism by Anthony Comstock (left) — a number of prominent suicides were traced to this vice crusader. To get the birth-control advocate Margaret Sanger back from England, Comstock had her estranged husband, William, jailed for her pamphlet *Family Limitation.* Many groups such as the National Liberal League tried in vain to stop this Comstockery, but he did himself in. Comstock died in 1915 from pneumonia resulting from a cold he caught at William Sanger's trial.

THE BEECHER AND TILTON

MRS. TILTON

H.W. BEECHER THEO. TILTON

WAR

PRICE 25 CENTS.

"Heavenly Marriage"

In the 1870s Henry Ward Beecher (1813–87), brother of Harriet Beecher Stowe and the era's most influential minister, arranged what he called a "heavenly marriage" with his lover, the thirty-five-year-old Elizabeth Tilton, and swore her to secrecy. She did tell her husband, Theodore Tilton, however, and he leaked the information to Victoria Woodhull, the noted free-lover who just happened to spend a lot of time with him. Woodhull waited for the right moment to use this juicy story, blackmailing Beecher into sponsoring her for an upcoming lecture at Steinway Hall. In private, Beecher admitted his acceptance of free love, but he did not show up at her event. Next she tried the court of public opinion. She called him a hypocrite and wrote that Elizabeth Tilton's love for Beecher was the true marriage, while her socially sanctioned union with Tilton was simply prostitution. Anthony Comstock, the city's protector of morals, got the feds to call this language equating marriage with prostitution obscene, and Woodhull was sent up the river.

The Girl in the Red Velvet Swing

Evelyn Nesbit (1884–1967) was in great demand as a photographer's model and an artist's muse. She sat for the artist Frederic Church and the rising illustrator Charles Dana Gibson. Between the ages of sixteen and twenty one, she miscarried the actor John Barrymore's child and was the mistress of New York's premier architect, Stanford White (1853–1906). The designer of the Washington Square arch, the Plaza Hotel, and the old Madison Square Garden, White was known to have a special desire to deflower young virgins. Nesbit would go to White's Twenty-fourth Street apartment and let him push her, naked, on a red velvet swing that hung from his high ceiling. Too old for White's taste, she married the loony millionaire Harry K. Thaw. When he saw White at a new musical at the architect's own Madison Square Garden on June 25, 1906, his insane rage over the allegation that White had debauched at least 278 virgins boiled over. He shot the architect in the head three times. Thaw's highly publicized trial ended in a hung jury. The second trial sent Thaw to Matteawan, home to the criminally insane, but the third found him sane. After having Thaw's son, Nesbit picked up with the dancer Jack Clifford, shocking audiences with their ragtime dances. She married him in 1916, and Thaw went back to the asylum for horsewhipping a young boy.

Self-Defense

On August 26, 1986, as the football player–sized Robert Chambers told police, Jennifer Levin, five feet four, tied him up with her panties and began to roughly fondle him. To halt this case of female rape, Chambers just had to kill her. The press played up Levin's party-girl, boy-crazy past while ignoring Chambers's drug and alcohol abuse, expulsions from school, and burglary attempts. The defense, by Jack T. Litman, blamed the victim. The famous prosecutor Linda Fairstein had already bumped up rape convictions to seventy-five percent since they had reached a low of ten percent in 1973. Chambers copped a plea of manslaughter and one burglary count, pleaded no contest to a $25 million civil suit by the Levins, and was up for parole in December 2002.

Long Island Lolita

New Yorkers loved this working-class sex scandal, trying to decide what was more appalling: a seventeen-year-old high school senior shooting her adult lover's wife in the head; a burley auto-body shop owner who had to plead guilty to statutory rape (and might have prodded his lovely Lolita to take out his wife), now a cable TV show host in L.A.; or a wife who forgave her attempted murderer, getting her sentence reduced and remaining with her philanderer-husband? Amy Fisher pleaded guilty to an assault shooting in 1992, was released in 1999, and dropped her $220 million lawsuit claiming that she was raped by five corrections officers while at Albion Correctional Facility in western New York.

SEX ED AND MED

Before the twentieth century, health problems in New York were blamed as much on the infestation of sin as on the filth in city streets. When cholera hit in 1832, evangelical ministers believed that it would pass over the virtuous parts of town, while God's wrath would strike at sinners. The road to health was the path of righteousness. In the early 1830s Sylvester Graham (1794–1851) lashed out against white bread, feather beds, pork, tobacco, salt, condiments, tight corsets, nocturnal emissions, heavy clothing, and hot mince pie. Masturbation and poor eating habits in particular, he reasoned, undercut the body's ability to fight disease. Certain maladies were passed through sexual acts, of course. Moralists promoting abstinence, who wanted to keep sex under wraps, battled health professionals and shrewd businesspeople who saw the need for public information and prophylaxis. Enter Margaret Sanger (1883–1966), a nurse and mother of three, who decided that by obtaining equality through birth control, women could change society. In her radical journal launched in 1914, *The Woman Rebel*, she covered women's sexual and reproductive anatomy as well as labor strife, marriage, and prostitution. Anthony Comstock banned some of her articles on sexual hygiene, and postal authorities told her to shut down. Instead, she packed all of the sex information into the pamphlet *Family Limitation*. Sanger fled to Europe, but her estranged husband was jailed for possession of the material. Leaving the sex psychologist Havelock Ellis, she came back to the States with so much support that the federal charges were dropped, lest she become a martyr. Before Sanger, feminists actually objected to contraceptives, contending that they did not fit in with ideals of motherhood and feminine virtue. 💗

Contradeception

With all the public sex available in New York, men and women needed a little protection. The 1873 Comstock law made contraception both illegal and obscene, but New Yorkers always got their hands on untested "sheaths," IUDs, pessaries, "womb veils," "male caps," douches, and other "hygiene" products. Condoms finally received the stamp of decency in 1918 — if prescribed by a doctor for disease prevention. Julius Schmid rode the wave of the booming condom industry in the 1930s with his lines of Ramses, XXXX (Fourex), Paradise, Velveto, and Sheik prophylactics. He went from making sausage cases by hand to mass producing a standardized, safe, and reliable condom, packaged in concealable tins and easier to get than by whispering to a druggist. In 1938 *Fortune* dubbed Julius Schmid of Queens "King of the American Condom Empire."

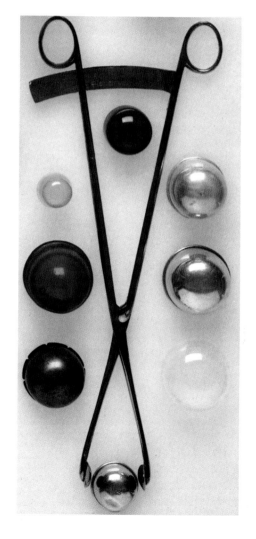

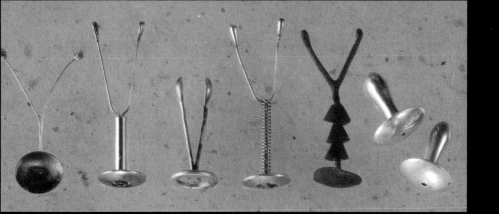

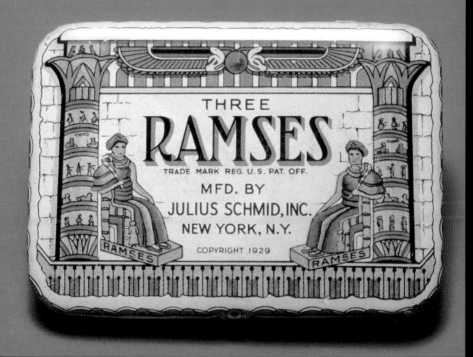

You kept fit
and defeated the Hun
Now—
set a high standard
A
CLEAN
AMERICA
!
STAMP OUT VENEREAL DISEASES-
21294
THE H.C. MINER LITHO. CO. N.Y.

The Grandmother of Sex Education

For a time American doughboys were the only forces abroad denied the use of condoms during World War I. Europeans tolerated men's needs, inspecting and licensing camp prostitutes, but Americans were expected to abstain. The New York–based American Social Hygiene Association, diverging from the more pragmatic

proponents fighting the spread of sex-based diseases, took a moralistic stance |on condom use. Franklin D. Roosevelt, then assistant secretary of the navy, had to covertly order remedies to cure the infections when seventy percent of U.S. soldiers were unable to "just say no." In the early 1960s Mary Steichen Calderone (1904–98), daughter of Edward Steichen and niece of Carl Sandburg, changed the approach to social hygiene, cofounding the Sexuality Information and Education Council of the United States (SIECUS) "to establish man's sexuality as a health entity . . . to dignify it by openness of approach, study and scientific research designed to lead toward its understanding and its freedom from exploitation."

Relieving Tension

For women who suffered "hysteria," "pelvic hyperemia," or "congestion of the genitalia," family physicians — given the late nineteenth century's prohibition of masturbation — did their duty to relieve the trouble with a little "vulvular massage" aimed at "hysterical paroxysm." With manual stimulation laborious and air- and steam-powered massagers expensive, doctors welcomed the assortment of electromechanical vibrators that came on the scene in the 1880s. Early vibrators were advertised in the Sears, Roebuck catalogue and magazines such as *Good Housekeeping* as a necessity for women's health. These devices were fifth in a line of household appliances to be electrified, after the sewing machine, fan, teakettle, and toaster. Warning: For external use only.

Surveying Sex

Katherine Bement Davis may have been the first female sexologist. Besides being a prison reformer and the first woman corrections commissioner for New York (1914), Davis surveyed single women about their erotic lives, including a study begun in 1920 of 2,200 women in the New York area. She sent questionnaires to 20,000 women who were "normal" or of good standing – mostly teachers and college graduates, aged twenty-five to fifty-five. Alfred Kinsey reportedly called her survey "simple, but statistical." The study found that more than half of single women and thirty percent of married women had experienced some degree of homosexual involvement. Other pioneering American sexuality surveys of women and marriage were made by Clelia Mosher (1891) and Anita Newcomb McGee (1888–91).

Sound Body, Sound Mind

Tony Sansone, a native New Yorker born in 1905, learned to make a beautiful and physically fit body through the Charles Atlas program and became one of the most desired artists' models of the 1920s and 30s. This living Greek statue was captured in classic style and light by the renowned New York physique photographer Edwin Townsend. Unlike earlier strongman photographs and the beefcake shots to come, these photographs portray a healthy artfulness. A dancer and an actor for a time, Sansone preferred to run his mail-order body-building system and gymnasiums around New York. The Italian American also self-published seminude photographs and booklets in the 1930s. The city's packed health clubs today attest to Sansone's concept that one way to be sexy is simply to be healthy.

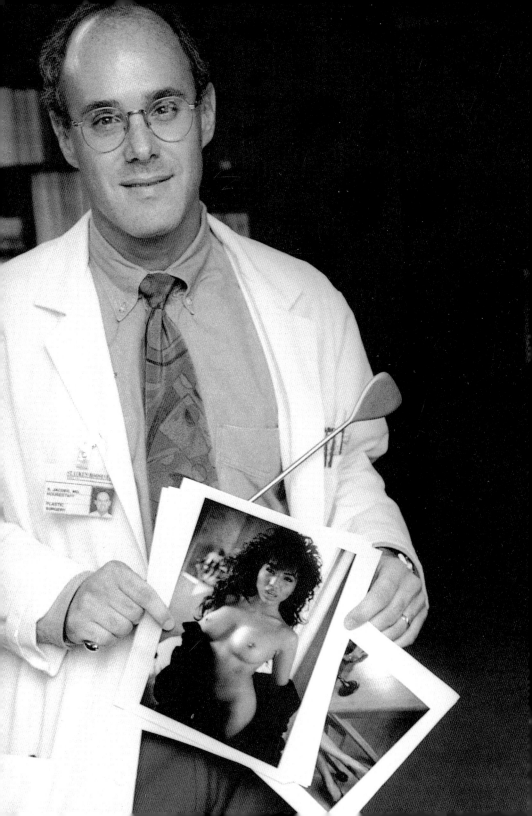

Occupational Expenses

Sex workers and dancers, especially those
over thirty-five, must constantly improve
their appearance, sometimes with new
shoes, hair, makeup, and tans and
sometimes with saline or size DD silicon.
Male dancers also need expensive surgery
and go for steroids on top. Dr. Brad Jacobs
has been a best friend to New York sex
workers, enhancing their bodies in a major
hospital's clinic and treating many without
health insurance for colds and the flu.
Now with a Park Avenue office, the doctor
continues to fix faces, butts, and bellies.
Regarding vaginas, "If things are a little
loose," he says, "we can tighten them up."

SCENE AND BE SEEN

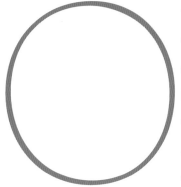

ther U.S. cities — San Francisco, Las Vegas, and New Orleans, for example — have reputations for fantastic sexual offerings. But because New York has always been the undisputed center of the free market and has rivaled European cities for first place in the arts, the city continues to be positioned as *the* place for free-wheeling sexual entertainment and wares. New York's generally libertarian spirit has always allowed for a good deal of public pleasures, from the wild Haymarket concert saloons and dime museums of the nineteenth century to the bawdy, male-oriented burlesque shows that welcomed their share of strippers in the 1920s to sex toy shops, gentlemen's clubs, and Chippendale shows for women. Of all these, one of the sexiest diversions in this wide-open town would have been a trip to see the most famous stripper ever: Gypsy Rose Lee (1914–70). After debuting in vaudeville at age four in 1918 and taking exotic dancing lessons from Tessie the Tassel Twirler in 1929, she was soon discovered by the burlesque impresario H. K. Minsky and eventually inspired the hit Broadway musical *Gypsy* (1959). She was a slow stripper. In three choruses, Gypsy might start with a little bump and grind, flirtatiously removing just her gloves and hat. In the tease section, she would unzip her breakaway dress, keeping it in front of her while she gyrated, always making sure that a hip, a leg, or a breast was alluringly visible. And the climax? A full strip down to a G-string, possibly the one made of mink, whose head bobbed up and down with her motions. Along with pasties on her nipples, these would be the only things standing between Gypsy Rose Lee and a trip to the station. ♥

"Whatever Lola Wants, Lola Gets"

Complete with whip, tarantula dance, and plenty of scandals, the vivacious, half-Spanish Lola Montez brought her passionate act to Broadway in 1851. The adoring audiences were mostly male, as ladies wouldn't risk the moral contamination of her dirty dancing. In her tarantula, the thirty-three-year-old Lola pretended to discover a hairy spider crawling on her body; as she frantically tried to knock it off, she loosened half of her clothes. When booed in Europe, she stripped off her garters and threw them to the audience. Soon crowds booed just to see this. She cracked the whip to beat off rowdy spectators. After success in San Francisco and a flopped play back in New York that sent her packing to the Bowery Theater, Lola died in relative obscurity in New York a decade later.

Wicked Shows

To Mark Twain, a tableau vivant was the
"wickedest show" on earth. Popularized in
the 1840s, tableaux vivants featured
"living statues" — somewhat uncouth
women in tights, diaphanous clothing, or
perhaps birthday suits — posing as figures
in paintings and classical sculpture.
Scenes usually depicted male ideals of
femininity, such as Mother Nature, the
seductress, or the ever-youthful
companions known as the *Three Graces*.
Some theaters had revolving stages, so
men could see the naughty bits every
now and then. When things got out of
hand in the 1850s, Mayor Fernando Wood
paraded the scantily clad gals down
Broadway to city hall. More sophisticated
tableaux vivants appealed to the elite as
symbols of great self-discipline.

Sinks of Iniquity

New Yorkers seeking some good clean family entertainment headed to dime museums such as P. T. Barnum's collection of man-made and natural curiosities. Less reputable museums along the Bowery (called "sinks of iniquity") leaned toward lurid spectacles of sexual deformities and crude entertainment, served liquor, and allowed prostitutes. The Bowery's Windsor Museum was always filled with teenage working girls, and the New Amsterdam Museum on Chatham Square was known for its prostitutes who wouldn't hesitate to pounce on men in their theater seats. And then at so-called anatomical museums, such as Dr. Wooster Beach's National Anatomical Museum and Academy of Natural Science, one might find "figures of men and women, naked, in lewd, lascivious, wicked, indecent, disquieting and obscene groups, attitudes and positions," according to the district attorney in 1850. Other attractions were models of reproductive organs and venereal diseases, stages of pregnancy, dissected breasts, hermaphrodites, a "Hottentot" female with an enlarged clitoris, and virgin breasts, "those rare beauties so peculiar to the female form, without which she would be despoiled of one half her elegance and loveliness."

GRAND ANATOMICAL MUSEUM,
No. 300 BROADWAY.

THIS IS THE MOST WONDERFUL AND GLORIOUS COLLECTION
Of ANATOMICAL MATTER in the World!

AN
Embalmed Body,

full size, exhibits all the organs from head to foot, and showing the MYSTERY and WONDER of our structure so perfectly, that every man exclaims in the language of the Psalmist,
"How wonderfully and fearfully are we made."

Queen of the Lobster Palace Days

Lillian Russell (1861–1922) could hit high Cs like no one else and had a curvaceous figure, glowing rosy complexion, sparkling smile, and queenly walk. No vamp or vixen, she reigned as America's beauty queen toward the end of the nineteenth century, starring at Weber and Field's Music Hall. Russell always made a memorable entrance at Martin's or Bustanoby's, perhaps with a gypsy fiddler playing one of her hit songs while she slowly moved down the main aisle, nodding and bowing left and right as she waltzed to her table. She might have met her friend, the well-heeled gourmand, "Diamond Jim" Brady, and his date, Edna McCauley, along with her own current lover, the millionaire Jesse Lewisohn. This foursome was inseparable – until Edna fell for Jesse when Jim had her nurse him when he was ill and Lillian was in Europe. After that Lillian and Jim had plenty of time to circle Central Park in their famous gilded and bejeweled bicycles. After she had been around a bit and gained a few pounds (long after this photograph was taken), Russell found herself in a lengthy lawsuit when she refused to wear tights while performing.

Maskers

How did anyone ever get anything done in nineteenth-century New York? Yet another utterly naughty thing to do was to attend one of the masquerade balls sponsored by prominent madams, politicians, and the Cercle Français de l'Harmonie (the most licentious masquerade party of them all after the Civil War). Even the Society for the Suppression of Vice held its own ball. While their faces were obscured, it was trés easy for mainstream New Yorkers to lose all inhibitions and push the bounds of public propriety (below). Others frequented early nightclubs, called concert saloons, that came on the scene in the 1840s, combining aspects of German beer garden, English theater, French vaudeville, and Italian opera. The biggest attraction was the "waiter girls," who wore low-cut bodices, very short skirts, and bare legs fitted with high tassled red boots and provided just about any service imaginable. Harry Hill's place on Houston, east of Broadway (above), had the distinction of being the "most reputable vile house" in town. He closed up after midnight and on Sundays and kept himself highly visible in church.

Finally, Something for the Ladies

In the early to mid-1800s, variety shows including singers, dancers, circus acts, and bawdy comics were widely employed in saloons and other makeshift entertainment venues. Guests were usually drunk and rowdy, so women and children stayed far away. Nudity and obscenity were prohibited, but sex was openly explored. "Blue acts" got audiences' attention. When Tony Pastor replaced variety shows with more sophisticated vaudeville, families from all strata of society flocked to see the quality acts. Eugene Sandow, then one of the strongest men in the world, was on stage in the 1890s at Koster and Bial's, the most famous variety house in New York, which moved from Twenty-third to Thirty-fourth Street. Although it appeared to be good clean fun, his almost-nude act finally offered the ladies a little titillation.

Slumming

To get away from the bourgeois world and reaffirm their belief that the working class was totally degenerate, middle-class men, and some women, headed down to the city's red-light districts. Sometimes guides would direct them to infamous dance halls, opium dens, whiskey saloons, fairy resorts, black-and-tan clubs, or other dens of iniquity. Toward the late 1800s, the Slide topped Billy McGlory's Armory Hall as the worst dive in town. After denouncing such vice, the Reverend Charles Parkhurst (1842–1933) went slumming, in disguise and with a private detective, to see it all firsthand. He went from one vice resort to another, asking to be shown an "even worse" sexual activity. A saloon song memorialized his tour: "Dr. Parkhurst on the floor / Playing leapfrog with a whore / Ta-ra-ra-Boom-de-ay / Ta-ra-ra-Boom-de-ay." Men were titillated and women disgusted, so a good time was had by all.

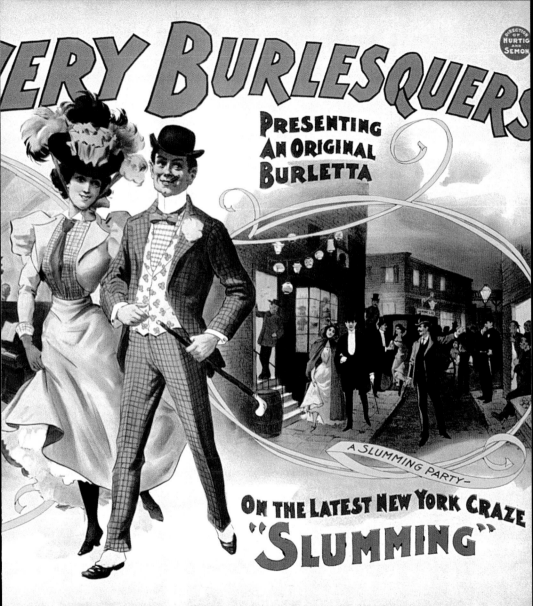

Insatiable Appetites

Ever since the Gilded Age — when elite restaurants such as Delmonico's, Sherry's, and the Hotel Savoy served some of the most satisfying comestibles in twelve courses to high society — New Yorkers have had a love affair with food. In downtown concert halls and eateries like Cavanagh's (below), "fairy" waiters, more than the food, were the draw. Flamboyantly effeminate men (known as sissies, she-men, nances, princesses, or duchesses) found working-class neighborhoods like the Bowery a great place to be themselves and make a buck giving services to the "trade" (straight men). In the 1890s *the* spot for male prostitutes was Columbia Hall, also known as Paresis (Insanity) Hall. For its abundant flamers, the Slide won the award for the most degenerate spot in the city. New York nightlife changed for good with the rise of the cabaret in the twentieth century's first decade. In these descendants of concert saloons, small tables encircled a large dance space, where teams performed and couples danced the Texas Tommy, Bunny Hop, and tango. A lot of sexually charged dancing went on, but the presence of prostitutes was played down. Murray's Roman Gardens on Forty-second Street (opposite) was one of the more elaborate, faithfully recreating a Caesarean villa in all its decadent grandeur.

New York's Moulin Rouge

The Haymarket on Sixth Avenue near Thirtieth Street, a glorified concert saloon in operation from the 1870s to 1910, was named after London's foremost prostitution quarter in the 1800s. (Sixth Avenue was known as New York's Haymarket.) Located in the legendary Satan's Circus, also called the Tenderloin, the "Moulin Rouge of New York" attracted a varied crowd, including the artist John Sloan (1871–1941) in 1907. "Diamond Jim" Brady (1856–1917) showed up sans his baubles. The saloon was one of a number of nineteenth-century entertainment venues — the Buckingham Palace, the Cremorne, the Cairo — named with European flair. Good style reigned outside and rules of propriety inside (no cheek-to-cheek dancing with prostitutes and no bare ankles), but the place was teeming with courtesans. The management was happy to provide special stalls for quick sex or naughty "circuses."

TAKE YOUR GIRLIE TO THE MOVIES

(IF YOU CAN'T MAKE LOVE AT HOME)

WORDS BY
**EDGAR LESLIE
& BERT KALMAR**

WATERSON
BERLIN
& SNYDER CO.
Music Publishers
Strand Theatre Bldg.
Broadway at 47th St.
NEW YORK

MUSIC BY
**PETE
WENDLING**

Palaces of Pleasure

With the premiere of movie theaters in the early
1900s, young men and women traded in their old leisure
activities — amusement parks, dance halls, and nickel
movie houses — for the dark and romantic palaces of
pleasure. Before sound films, piano music helped set the
tone for holding hands, kissing, and groping, especially
in the notorious back rows. Feature films with beautiful,
romantic, suave, and sensual actors gave them an
education and a taste of passion and encouraged
independence. Before the Hays Code (1934), many films
had erotic or suggestive scenes, and even the early silent
films ignored taboos, projecting lawlessness, drug use,
prostitution, and religious blasphemy. Films like *Kiss*
(1896); *Sin* (1915), with the original vamp, Theda Bara;
Cecil B. DeMille's *Male and Female* (1919); and Rudolf
Valentino's *Sheik* (1921) attracted big crowds. Young men
who could afford it treated young women to movies and
other amusements, further defining the role of men as
provider of things in exchange for sexual favors.

All-American Follies

The legendary showman Florenz "Flo" Ziegfeld
(1869–1932) reworked the Parisian Folies Bergère in 1907
to suit American tastes. Following the recipe for skits, songs,
and commentary on the social and political follies of the
day, Ziegfeld made the productions New York–lavish, with
top composers and seminude displays, all aimed at "The
Glorification of the American Girl." Ziggy's girls — among
them Louise Brooks, Josephine Baker, Barbara Stanwick,
Lana Turner, Paulette Goddard, Ruby Keeler, and Gypsy
Rose Lee — were dubbed "the most beautiful girls in the
world." They shared the stage with W. C. Fields, Bert
Williams, Will Rogers, Eddie Cantor, and Fanny Brice.
Fashions by Lady Duff-Gordon and Erté dramatically
decorated the feminine forms. The pinup artist Alberto
Vargas (1896–1982) was commissioned beginning in
1919 to paint the stars of the Follies, which he did for
the next twelve years. All in all, it was a respectable girlie
show to which a man could bring his wife.

DO THE NEW YORK
by J. P. MURRAY, BARRY TRIVERS AND BEN OAKLAND
ZIEGFELD FOLLIES
GLORIFYING THE AMERICAN GIRL
LYRICS AND MUSIC BY
J. P. MURRAY
BARRY TRIVERS
BEN OAKLAND
MACK GORDON
HARRY REVEL
GENE BUCK
DAVE STAMPER
AND OTHERS
PUBLISHED BY
MILLER MUSIC
INCORPORATED
62 WEST 45TH ST. N.Y.C.
ALBERTO VARGAS
STAGED BY BOBBY CONNELLY
HERE WE ARE IN LOVE
WRAPPED UP IN YOU
DO THE NEW YORK
CIGARETTES, CIGARS!
LET'S K'NOCK K'NEES

Khaki-Wackies

What has more erotic appeal than a man in uniform? The Chinese pin-up queen Noel Toy showed her appreciation to this seaman in 1945. During World War II other young women, faced with a tremendous man shortage, were more than willing to do a little something for their country. Moral crusaders turned their attention from prostitutes to the good-time Charlottes and victory girls. To GIs, gonorrhea was the least of their worries. Once abroad, servicemen got used to new sexual styles, such as the Japanese technique of baths and massages before intercourse. Not so well accepted in some states were Japanese wives of black or white men. Gays, especially, enjoyed their new sex-segregated worlds, whether all-male barracks or all-female boarding houses and women's corps. Although many heterosexuals headed to picture-perfect family lives in the suburbs after the war, the social and sexual freedoms that had been won expanded until they exploded in the 1960s.

Bump and Grind, Strip and Tease

When burlesque (from the Italian *burla,* meaning jest) had to get racy to compete with family-style vaudeville and Ziegfeld's Follies, bump-and-grind queens like Evelyn West, Tempest Storm, and Lili St. Cyr did the trick, playing Times Square theaters. St. Cyr

(1918–99) was known for her flying G-string act (whereby a fishing rod offstage yanked off her cover just before the lights went down), taking bubble baths, and being dressed by a maid on-stage. She took her act to the silver screen in films such as Irving Klaw's *Varietease* (1954). From the 1940s to the 50s, her erotic ballet act helped her dethrone Gypsy Rose Lee and Ann Corio as queens of the striptease. The "bur-le-q" survived Mayor Fiorello LaGuardia's ban in 1937, and Scores, the gentlemen's club on East Sixtieth Street (opposite), likewise outlasted Mayor Rudolph Giuliani's crackdown on commercial sex. High class and high cost, the club boasts beautiful ladies, a cigar humidor, and a restaurant, although its main bill of fare is typical strip joint: almost-nude ladies bumping and grinding on stage, lap dancing, and hosting private parties. Special individual bathroom stalls help relieve pressures of all sorts (the attendants are well tipped).

DEMIMONDAINES

t might be inconceivable that sex was ever more in evidence than it is today in New York, but during the Victorian era — when outward expressions of sexuality were not tolerated by polite society — prostitution was a major part of the city landscape. The nineteenth century was New York's golden age of prostitution. A vital part of the city's economy, it was tolerated by the police and city government, working-class men, many of New York's bourgeois males, and women who were told that it was a good outlet for men who would otherwise compromise the virtue of decent women. At midcentury, Dr. William Sanger estimated that annual revenues from commercial sex exceeded $3 million annually; with liquor sales and income from rent, the figure fell just under that of the garment industry. Although prostitution wasn't all rosy by any means, being "on the job" was a good way for women to become financially and socially independent. It could be said that the city was built partially on the backs of women. Prostitution remains today, from streetwalkers to massage-parlor workers to high-class call girls, but its illegal status necessitates that it be surreptitious and kept to remote areas. Even the most secretive places in New York, of course, can be in the sightlines of millions of people. The photographer Merry Alpern spent the blizzardy winter of 1993–94 in a friend's Wall Street apartment, focusing across the alley on what she calls her characters in an office bathroom minidrama whose props included condoms, tattoos, silicone, and crack (opposite). She was never found out, but the show got canned by the local cops. ❤

Hot Corners for Hooking a Victim

· Corlears Hook, near the shipyards
· East River, along Cherry, Water, and Walnut Streets
· Five Points
· Rotten Row, along Church and Chapel Streets north of Canal Street
· SoHo
· The Tenderloin, along Sixth Avenue from Twenty-third to Fifty- seventh Street
· Soubrette Row on West Thirty-ninth Street
· African Broadway, up Seventh Avenue from Twenty-third to Fortieth Street
· The Rialto, on Fourteenth Street from Third Avenue to Union Square and Broadway
· Bleeker Street and Washington Square
· Broadway between Madison Square and Longacre (later Times) Square
· Forty-second Street

Don't Go There

Ostensibly reproachful exposés of New York's sexual underworld, guidebooks such as A. Butt Ender's *Prostitution Exposed* (1839) could actually give a guy a good time. Using statistics from the New York Female Moral Reform Society, this early form of pornography, available at newsstands, described where to find the city's most tempting brothels. The madams running them were some of the most financially independent people in the city by the 1840s. Rosina Townsend became a household name after the murder of Helen Jewett in her highly regarded City Hotel brothel. The sporting press also put the spotlight on Celeste Thebault, Ann Thompson, Jane Williams, and especially Rebecca "Lady" Williams, who could have fooled anyone when she shopped at A. T. Stewart's Marble Emporium. It was said that Sophia "La Belle" Austin's excellent brothel was "orderly and supported by chaps who do such business in the dark." In 1896 the Raines Law — designed to restrict prostitution — specified that only hotels with ten or more beds could serve alcohol on Sunday. Saloonkeepers dutifully added bedrooms, in the bargain helping prostitutes find clients. Rosie Hertz, the "godmother for prostitutes," and her husband, Jacob, became rich from five brothels and Raines Law hotels along East First Street.

Although they had been in business since the 1880s, they had to pay dearly for police protection after 1905, and they ultimately lost their fortune, with Rosie doing a year for graft. The Raines Law destroyed dining out for respectable fin-de-siècle New Yorkers.

FIFTH EDITION—WITH MANY ADDITIONS.

PROSTITUTION EXPOSED;

OR, A

MORAL REFORM DIRECTORY,

LAYING BARE THE

Lives, Histories, Residences, Seductions, &c.

OF THE MOST CELEBRATED

COURTEZANS AND LADIES OF PLEASURE

OF THE CITY OF NEW-YORK,

Together with a Description of the Crime and its Effects,

AS ALSO, OF THE

Houses of Prostitution and their Keepers,

HOUSES OF ASSIGNATION,

THEIR CHARGES AND CONVENIENCES,

AND OTHER PARTICULARS INTERESTING TO THE PUBLIC.

BY A BUTT ENDER.

NEW-YORK:

PUBLISHED FOR PUBLIC CONVENIENCE,

1839.

Princess Julia

Some courtesans such as Julia Brown and Kate Ridgely continued to operate their thriving businesses for ten years at a stretch. Brown (opposite), a renowned antebellum prostitute, had many admirers — some say that even Dickens visited her while in America in 1842. Her resplendent "two thousand dollar" parlor house on Leonard Street was furnished with the same stylish chairs found in the National Theater, which burned down and ruined part of one of her other brothels. She could often be seen at grand balls and parties given by the elite of Bleeker Street. Others saw her dark side: as a greedy extortionist of her working-girl boarders. One former prostitute who could not claw her way back into society was Eliza Bowen Jumel, who married the prosperous French wine merchant Stephen Jumel in the early 1800s. Even after a ten-year stay in France, where she became highly respected, she was excluded from New York high society.

Truth Greater Than Fiction?

New York's spicy underground has seeped into the city's literature and art over the centuries. In antebellum stories, the prostitute and the madam became main characters. Dime novelists such as Ned Buntline made fictional accounts "drawn from real life," in which, according to Timothy Gilfoyle, "New York is a city of extremes, where the forces of civilization met those of savagery, represented by innocent virginity and sexual promiscuity." George Foster, who exposed the city in *New York by Gaslight* (1850), gave readers dramatic realism, writing about real-life women on the town, madams, and abortionists. Courtesans were rarely approved of, often portrayed as mad, devilish tricksters who victimized men. Pictures in George Ellington's *Women of New York* (1869) (opposite) actually depicted some "gay girls" as almost respectable ladies. For many women who had a hard time finding a place to live in the city, brothels and dual-purpose boarding houses filled a need, as Reginald Marsh documented in his 1928 print *Brothel* (above).

The Real Yellow Peril

A slumming craze in the late nineteenth and early twentieth centuries took audacious New Yorkers into the mysterious world of Chinatown, located in the infamously squalid Sixth Ward, to visit chop suey houses, Joss houses, opium dens, Chinese theater, and fan-tan gambling parlors. "Chinamen," who were always seen as a threat to white men's economic status on the West Coast, headed to New York after the building of the transcontinental railroad in 1869. Here they created an almost exclusively male culture. The Chinese Exclusion Act of 1882 made it even harder for men to bring over wives, and many married Irish "apple women." Because the Chinese culture was filled with exotic smells and strange sights and sounds, not to mention the Chinese criminal element, New Yorkers considered Chinatown an evil place that could trap white women. Even secondhand smoke from opium, it was feared, would threaten the morals of adolescent girls, causing them to lose all modesty and self-control. In June 1909 Elsie Sigel, who was purportedly working as a missionary, was found murdered in a trunk in the apartment of two Chinese men. The cartoonist Robert Carter dubbed the scenario "The Real Yellow Peril," underscoring the view that white women, rather than men, were the ones really at risk from oriental men.

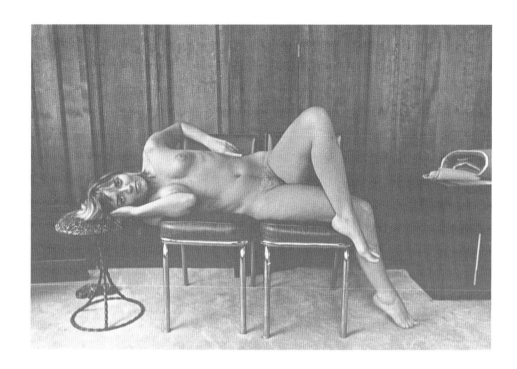

The Happy Hooker

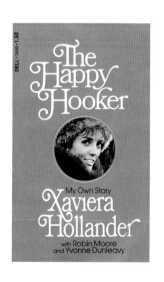

Voted Holland's best secretary in the late 1960s, Xaviera de Vries, a.k.a. Xaviera Hollander, headed to New York to become secretary to the Dutch consul and later to the Belgian ambassador. To augment her salary, she joined a call-girl agency and then invested $10,000 in a retiring madam's client list. The rest is happy-hooking history, as revealed in her bestselling 1971 memoir. "Call Me Madam," she has told *Penthouse* readers for thirty years. Now she entertains friends and the public with English theater productions and elaborate dinners in her Amsterdam home.

The Mayflower Madam

Sydney Biddle Barrows, a descendant
of Mayflower pilgrims, cared enough for
her girls to offer them a health plan.
Nevertheless, her classy call-girl ring for
rich and powerful men, Cachet, was raided
in 1984, leading to her arrest. Type A
clients, who found Cachet through
domestic ads, were charged $125 to $175
an hour, while B clients, readers of the
International Herald Tribune, were hit for
$135 to $195. C girls — blond, buxom,
and under twenty-five — filled requests
for even "more beautiful" women and
came for $450 a two-hour session.
Barrows went on to write *Mayflower
Manners: Etiquette for Consenting Adults*
(1990) and married Darney Hoffman,
Bernhard Goetz's lawyer.

A League of Her Own

Inspired as a young girl by the Happy Hooker, Tracy Quan set out to be a *Playboy* centerfold or a prostitute, but her interest in "collecting fines" (like librarians) sent her into the trade. With her exotic (Trinidadian and Chinese) good looks, she started hustling in her early teens. After learning the ropes in London champagne bars, Quan returned to New York and joined an escort service, finally going with a high-class madam. Of her three thousand clients, many were businessmen who wanted to satisfy their appetites at lunchtime with doubles and multiples. She told all in her fictionalized *Diary of a Manhattan Call Girl* (2001). Now Quan works with Prostitutes of New York (PONY), established in the 1970s to push for decriminalization of prostitution.

Equal Opportunity

Times Square in the 1920s was full of
fairies and "go-getters" who attracted
sailors. After the repeal of Prohibition in
1933, gay bars proliferated, and by the
1950s male hustlers were usually on
Forty-second Street between Seventh
and Eighth Avenues – "The Deuce."
From the 1960s to the 1980s, a seamy
circus of sex workers, johns, grifters, and
unusual characters took over. A hustler
named Silver stands in front of the
renovated Roxy Theater, a burlesque-sex
club-turned-quad sex cinema on the
infamous street. Not all hustlers are gay.
Homosexual or bisexual, they get into
the business, full or part-time, for the
dough. Many think that they are not
actually having sex when they give or
get blow jobs or perform sex acts on a
john. Some practice safe sex. For hustlers,
drugs are usually the biggest risk.

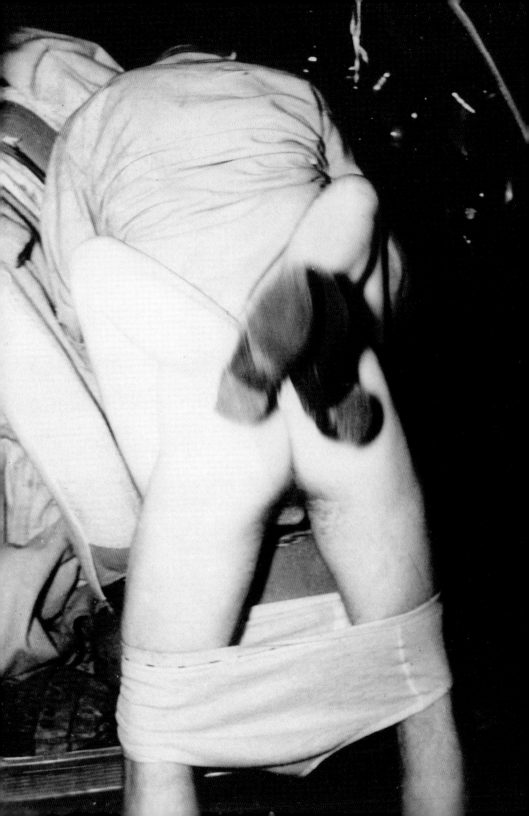

E S C A P E S

Stalwart New Yorkers hate the thought of leaving their city of cities, center of the universe. But full of energy — the daily hustle, millions of people, things to do, buy, and see all crammed into countless square boxes that constitute the city blocks — New York is a pressure cooker. If it weren't for the knowledge that escapes are possible, no one would survive. Escaping the city also means escaping from civilization: rules, conventions, parental and workplace controls, prying neighbors, gawking crowds. Manhattan went from a city to a metropolis between 1823 and 1860. Masses of immigrants filled up the city, moving into stifling quarters and working monotonous jobs for hours on end. More than ever, the need for escape became urgent. In the 1830s, and even more so in the 1870s, as transportation got better, New Yorkers began heading to Arcadian Coney Island and nearby Central Park to restore the senses. Both offered a little isolation from the city. Virgin nature set the scene for a bit of romance and lust. When Henry Ford greatly speeded up production of the new automobile around 1913, he made affordable not only escape from the city, but also a diversion in its own right. Cars were and are machines of escape, carrying riders far from the predictability of everyday life to exciting locations and promising great privacy (with some exceptions, such as a 1940s couple found out). For youths, these independence mobiles, broadening freedoms and full of sexual possibilities, represent an important transition to adulthood. ♥

Fast Women in Central Park

Central Park, New York's in-town rural pleasure ground designed by Frederick Law Olmsted and Calvert Vaux over two decades beginning in 1858, has been a major social center and 843-acre hideout for amorous activity. All strata of society used the park. The mall was the site of ladies' afternoon walks and many attempts at courtship. This urban oasis was one place sanctioned for a young woman and a young man to meet unchaperoned. Celebrity demimondaines from the Louvre Concert Saloon and refined fancy brothel owners such as Josephine Wood frequently made appearances in their impressive carriages, as did the abortionist Madame Restelle, whose carriage was a match for that of any of the city's grand dowagers.

Reginald Marsh 1943

Seeing the Elephant

In 1869 the railroad finally made Coney Island accessible to enervated city workers. It was a pleasure zone (called by the architect Rem Koolhaas the "clitoral appendage at the entrance of New York Harbor"), with great beaches, amusements, and even a Tenderloin "lite" on the island's west end. A visit to the giant elephant-shaped restaurant was a must see – the phrase "seeing the elephant" came to mean a hunt for all of the naughty pleasures in sleazy areas. The Tunnel of Love in Luna Park took unfamiliar couples in small boats into dark grottoes where, to the sexy swishing sound of the boat rocking on the water, they could have some unchaperoned quality time. At the Barrel of Love, men and women entered two huge revolving barrels from separate entrances at either end. No one could remain standing, so they fell all over each other.

Comin' Out of Hiding

Gays have claimed a number of city and suburban spaces for their own. The Piers, adjacent to the Hudson River waterfront in the West Village, and specifically the Christopher Street Pier (number 45), became a rough resort for gays, queens, homeless kids, and other social outsiders after the 1960s. Mayor Rudolph Giuliani fenced off the nighttime-crime arena in the late 1990s to build the Hudson River Park, where at least thongs are legal. Fire Island, a barrier beach on Long Island's south shore, has been the summer capital of the gay world since the mid-twentieth century. The Pines and Cherry Grove have huge gay communities, which are known for their sweaty, packed, hard-bodied parties throughout the summer.

otham has always had plenty of cracks and crevices in its imposing grid and as many people who sneak into them to find a safe haven. Marginalized groups, from African Americans to gays, radical intellectuals and artists, and sexual fetishists, have made their niches in bars, clubs, restaurants, and whole areas of the city. Many of them took the "A" train to Harlem in the 1920s to enjoy the nightlife and jazzy black American music. Here in the home of the Harlem Renaissance people could express their sexual proclivities, living "in the life." In Jazz Age Harlem, art met sexual license for a wide array of public and private performances. Many key figures of the Harlem Renaissance, especially in music — Bessie Smith, Ma Rainey, and the 300-pound singer Gladys Bentley, known for her white tux and top hat — brought homosexual innuendo (and overtly obscene lyrics) to their adoring fans. White progressives loved Harlem's freedom and could be found at local rent parties and costume balls. The latter were glorious homosexual events where men dressed up like senoritas, soubrettes, and debutantes. The premier photographer of the African American community, James VanDerZee, made a portrait of one extravagantly dressed beau of the ball (opposite). Gawkers could get box seats in places such as the Savoy Ballroom to watch the magnificent parade of unashamed mock divas. Harlem was not unlike another home of creative freedom and sexual trends: Greenwich Village, the downtown haven for men and women wishing to do as they pleased, with whomever they pleased. These free zones continue to keep the city electrifyingly on the edge of culture. ♥

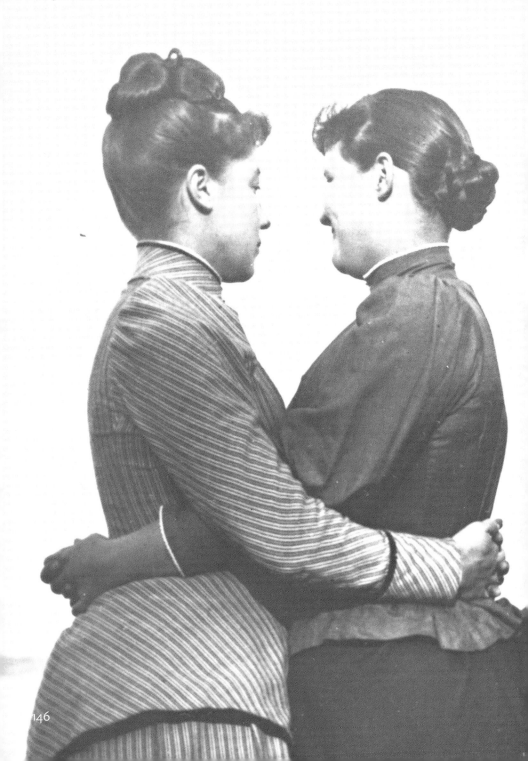

In 1905 New York was home to many never-married women — academics, labor organizers, and social workers — who lived with other women. The Membership of Heterodoxy, a Greenwich Village women's political club, recorded quite a few pairs of "devoted companions" as members. As a code, they wore heavy woolen suits, even in the summer.

Steamy Situations

Sodomy was banned in New York's earliest days. In 1646 Jan Creoli, a black man, was convicted of a second offense and sentenced to death by choking and then "burned to ashes." Manuel Congo, the ten-year-old whom Creoli allegedly sodomized, received a public flogging. Beginning in the early twentieth century, bathhouses provided safe spaces for gay males to have sex as well as to develop friendships and romance. Unaffected by outsiders in the baths, gays were freer to be themselves. Unlike the public or religious baths, the Turkish or Russian baths — where the body was treated as a temple — usually tolerated gay men or converted to totally gay bathhouses. In world-famous spots such as the Everhard on West Twenty-eighth Street and the Lafayette Baths, frequented by the artist Charles Demuth, and even Stauch's on Coney Island, men could have sex in the murky steam rooms or in crowded, open cooling rooms full of cots, or they would simply make dates for later. Mount Morris in Harlem, the longest-running bath (overlooked by the city's 1985 anti-AIDS measure), was the only house that admitted blacks until the 1960s. With sodomy technically illegal until recently, raids on bathhouses were frequent.

In or Out

Gays developed extensive subcultures by the mid-twentieth century, but they remained inhibited by social pressures and Cold War sensibilities. The first gay bars opened in the 1940s, including a few for daring lesbians. Two women posturing in a bar caught the attention of the famous New York underworld photographer Weegee (Arthur Fellig)

(1899–1968). Around this time, these gals might have been called Kikis, diesel dykes, collar-and-ties, slacks, majors, or Amy-Johns. The erotic energy in bars still seemed scary for women in that era, so most preferred private apartment parties. Men could cruise certain streets and parks, but — viewed as a threat to national security — they were better off at home.

Shaking It in Harlem

A certain type of burlesque, closer to vaudeville, could be found in Harlem after World War II. Performed in black-and-tan clubs to mixed races and mixed sexes, the shows — as captured in the 1950 film *Burlesque in Harlem,* directed by William Alexander — were full of skits with sexual innuendo, tap dancing, large ladies singing and making sexual jokes, even naughty dancing, and of course high-kicking, fringe-flying cooch dances. Tarza Young, Gloria Howard, and Princess D'Orsay were star strippers. These ladies shook their stuff like there was no tomorrow, but they never went so far as to offend the ladies in the audience.

Indecent Exposure

What a difference a decade makes. In the 1960s men who simply dressed up in women's clothes — for example, at the National Variety Artists Exotic Carnival and Ball — were locked up on charges of masquerading and indecent exposure. By contrast, the 1970s were the age of promiscuity, a time when a meat-packing plant-turned-infamous leather sex palace named the Mineshaft thrived. With a bar upstairs, a back room full of slings and glory holes, and golden showers in the basement, the after-hours club for gay S&M'ers lasted until 1985, when sex in commercial places was strictly prohibited.

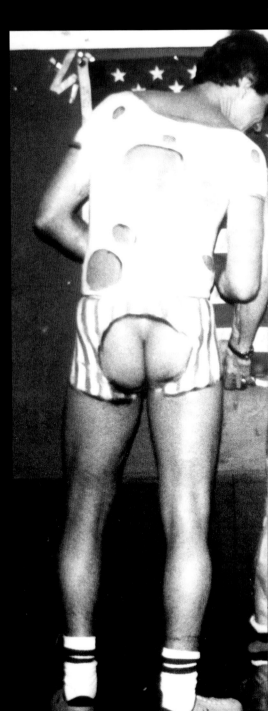

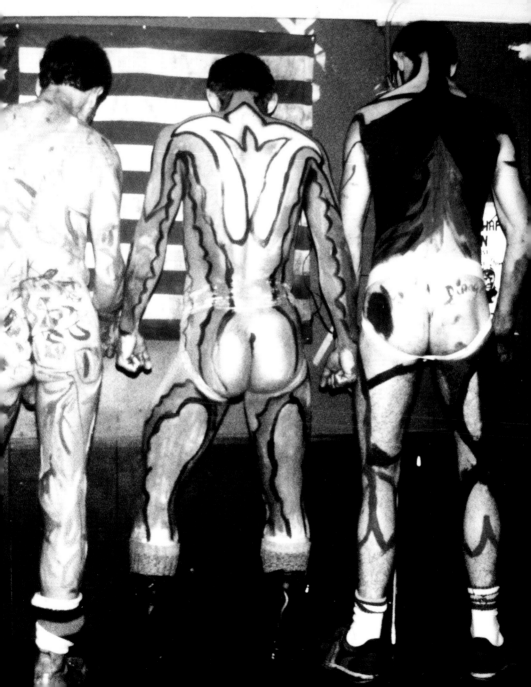

Although the city's fast-paced life is erotic in its own way, New Yorkers and tourists continue to spend their time and dollars on sex, pictures of sex, explicit stories (real and fiction), sex accoutrements, and things to make one sexy. Before the 1920s obscene materials were sold under the table or under pretense (remember Comstock). Sensational, romantic, forbidden, thrill-filled dime novels and pulp papers, which grew out of the story papers and cheap romances of the 1830s, were hot items in relatively public view. With a new economy, in which corporations needed consumers but didn't need as much round-the-clock labor, the erotic became more integrated into public life. Women were sold an ethic of consumption — told to buy things to ensure personal allure — and men had more leisure time to focus on the fun stuff. After War World II the porn and other products that had kept men happy on tour made their way to America. A new magazine genre, encompassing *He*, published in New York, and later *Playboy*, full of pinups and kinky photos, hit the newsstands. For gay men, "physical fitness" magazines, showcasing beefy bodies, did the trick. And for women? A little drama. Mix some romance, outrageous stories, and misadventures of Hollywood celebrities, and 1950s scandal magazines such as *Confidential*, another rag published out of New York, and *Keyhole* provided it. ♥

Retail Gyp: Small Things In Big Packages

SEE PAGE 24

PDC

Confidential ®

APRIL

Still 25¢

MONTHLY

Louisiana's Sex Scandal:
WHAT'S IN THAT SUPERSONIC TONIC, GOVERNOR?

TV's Perry Mason Gets Fooled:

THE CASE OF THE MISS WHO WAS A MISTER-Y

The First Family Has In-Law Trouble:

WHY PETER LAWFORD'S MA HATES JACK KENNEDY'S PA

SEE PAGE 20

JOSEPH P. KENNEDY

PETER LAWFORD

LADY LAWFORD

A STREET VIEW.

NUISANCES.—There are a number of nuisances at present existing in this city which should be abated. Look at the horrible situation of that poor female, and behold her agonized countenance. Years will not efface the remembrance of the occurrence from her mind, or soothe the pangs inflicted by that hog. Hog! We saw the accident; but can't recollect whether it was a sow or a boar. Because we didn't look. Rather guess the lady thought it was a very great bore! Hogs or boars are nuisances. We have seen apple-carts upset,—dandies ditto, white pants victimized, women knocked—*down*, and all sorts of crimes committed by hogs. They ought not to be allowed to run in the open streets—so said the lady—so said the gallant who officiated—so say we.

We will here take the opportunity to speak of another crying evil or nuisance. We have seen men, time and again, eye a fence or dead-wall very wistfully then walk up to it, pretend to read some poster, fum-

ble about a little while and then turn away, looking very red and confused. We have noticed a change in the fence or wall afterwards, and heard the little boys request the individual so doing, not "to set that are house afire." Then the individual thus addressed would either tell the said little boys to "go to h—ll," or pretend not hear it, and walk off as fast as his precious pins could carry him. It must be a nuisance, because we have never observed females to transact such business in the streets, and what is a monopoly is a nuisance.

Yet such nice things are permitted, while we, who possess the honest fearlessness to speak the truth and shame the devil, are annoyed, reviled and insulted. Well, consistency is one thing—gammon another. You will look at real dirty street exhibitions, pay high to gaze upon a disgusting dancer (?), yet you will speak against the embellishment before you, which is but ink and paper. It's all right.

The Weekly Rake.

Fellow Journalism

Even before the mid-nineteenth century, prostitutes and sporting men were changing New York's social structure. After the penny press, including the *New York Herald*, prospered wildly from its intense coverage of the murder of the prostitute Helen Jewett in 1836, other papers and journals devoted to prostitution and male sexual freedom sprang up. The most sensational were newspapers such as *The Rake, Whip, Flash, Libertine, Venus Miscellany,* and the long-running *Police Gazette,* which defended their licentious stories on the underworld as a way to force society to see its true self. These papers were part of a booming sexual commerce that included prostitution, abortion, pornography, and masculine-oriented sexual entertainment. On July 16, 1842, *The Whip* explained to readers that it was "Devoted to the Sports of the Ring, the Turf, and City Life — such as Sprees, Larks, Crim., Cons', Seductions, Rapes &c. — not forgetting to keep a watchful eye on all Brothels and their frail inmates; in fact, a paper that every one cannot fail to be pleased with, and will not relinquish until finished." As might be expected, the sporting press also regularly offered information on cures for VD.

Vice vs. Virtue

At the turn of the twentieth century,
paperbacks and Broadway melodramas
about virginity, its imminent loss, and
daring rescues entertained masses looking
for excitement, romance, and escape.
Most holdover Victorian stories, imported
from Europe, contained scandalous
situations that ended as virtue triumphed.
Covers on these 25-cent dime novels, like
New York by Night and *The King of Bigamists*,
grabbed people's attention with bold
graphics drawn from the flamboyant,
sexually suggestive advertising then on the
rise. In the race between vice and virtue,
as Oscar Wilde once chided a New York
audience, the wise money is on vice.

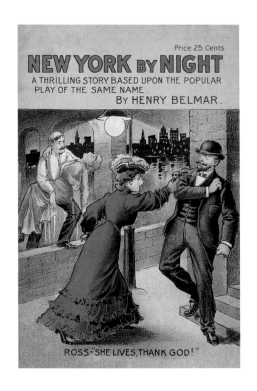

Price 25 Cents

THE KING OF BIGAMISTS

A STORY FOUNDED UPON A. H. WOOD'S PLAY OF THE SAME NAME.

By THEODORE KREMER.

NOVELIZED BY

OLIVE HARPER.

"THAT MAN IS A BIGAMIST, I AM HIS WIFE."

Smokin'

Cigar smoking became a big hit during the Civil War, as photographs of General Ulysses S. Grant testify. Before the war, cigars were sold as singles or in bundles of twenty-five or fifty, and buyers took what they got. When the government came up with the bright idea to tax these hot sellers, cigars had to be boxed, sealed, and stamped to ensure quality. Competition became fierce in the early 1870s, so boxes containing up to a hundred stogies were branded and left open for inspection in cigar shops and saloons. To lure customers, cigar makers added brilliant labels to the inside lids. Special themes abounded, from trains and ships to hunting and fishing, the West, science, politics, and patriotism, but most boxes were lined with pictures of beautiful women, including the requisite winged ladies and Indian maidens.

A Lot of Flap

The flapper — the young, smart woman who "knows the art of feminine appeal" (as a 1924 advertisement announced), wore hot red lipstick, had bobbed hair, smoked, drank, and petted — emerged during World War I. Realizing that the flapper ideal influenced young women, the advertising industry from Madison Avenue to Hollywood flaunted her image to fuel the American consumer economy in the 1920s. Ads like this one in *The Cosmopolitan,* directed toward women, really sold desire, not products, so the flapper was the perfect pitch. Women of the era nonetheless usually traded in sexual liberation for a husband and a house, after which their winking days were supposed to be over.

SACRED PROSTITUTION

AND

MARRIAGE BY CAPTURE

G. S. WAKE

Trading in Taboo

Underground erotic publishing (opposite) catalogued bizarre lusts in the 1920s and 30s. Typical tales, rooted in an old white-slavery scare, were terrifying accounts of black men capturing white women for prostitution or "marriage." Samuel Roth (above) helped make New York the erotica capital of the world. In the late 1920s he began publishing risqué literature such as long extracts of *Ulysses* (1914) without James Joyce's permission. Roth eventually had to further the cause of free speech in jail. A federal court in New York finally lifted the veil of censorship on Joyce's masterpiece in 1933.

Kiddie Porn

The illegal *Tijuana Bible* comic strips —
neither from the sin-ridden Mexican
border town nor very virtuous — were
published from the 1930s to the 1950s.
Available at typically male hangouts
around the city, these veritable sex-
education manuals using popular
characters and celebrities were highly
stylized — exaggerated just like other
comics and most porn. The creator of the
1939 World's Fair series, the New York
comic artist Wesley Morse, went on to
pen *Bazooka Joe,* the famous comic
wrapped around bubble gum.

EROS

Summer, 1962

With Intent to Porn

In *Ginzburg vs. the United States* (1965), the U.S. Supreme Court ruled that even though Ralph Ginzburg's publications — the artful *Eros* magazine, a newsletter aimed at "keeping sex an art and preventing it from becoming a science," and an "auto-biography," *The Housewife's Handbook on Selective Promiscuity* — had some redeeming social value, the fact that he pandered, or advertised that he was selling very sexy stuff, got him five years. The added fact that Ginzburg attempted to mail his wares and advertisements from Blue Ball and Intercourse, Pennsylvania, and Middlesex, New Jersey, gave prosecutors an edge.

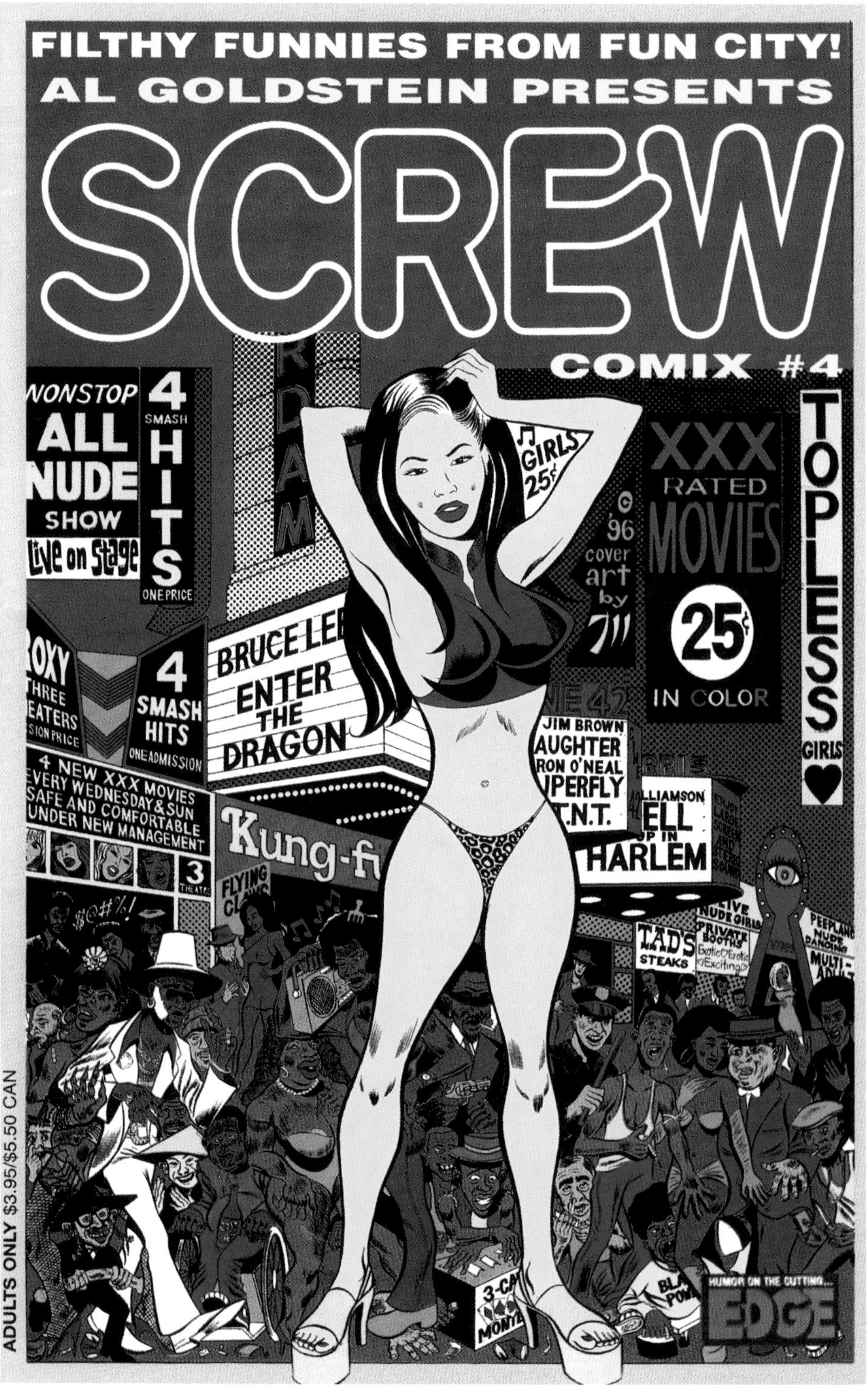
FILTHY FUNNIES FROM FUN CITY!
AL GOLDSTEIN PRESENTS
SCREW
COMIX #4
NONSTOP
ALL NUDE SHOW
Live on Stage
4 SMASH HITS
ONE PRICE
GIRLS 25¢
XXX RATED MOVIES
25¢
IN COLOR
© '96 cover art by
TOPLESS
GIRLS
4 SMASH HITS
ONE ADMISSION
BRUCE LEE
ENTER THE DRAGON
4 NEW XXX MOVIES
EVERY WEDNESDAY & SUN
SAFE AND COMFORTABLE
UNDER NEW MANAGEMENT
Kung-fu
JIM BROWN
RON O'NEAL
T.N.T.
HARLEM
TAD'S STEAKS
PRIVATE BOOTHS
3-CARD MONTE
HUMOR ON THE CUTTING...
EDGE
ADULTS ONLY $3.95/$5.50 CAN

Pop Sex

Al Goldstein launched *Screw* magazine in 1968 with a First Amendment credo: to "be the *Consumer Reports* of sex, we promise never to ink out a pubic hair or chalk out an organ, [we'll] give sex a break and make no bones about it. People fuck and do other things to each other . . . we'll lay it on the line, and on the bed, and floor, until the whole world gets the art." Goldstein created adults-only *Screw Comix* twenty-five years after unleashing his list of hip-to-be-horny publications. The artist of the cover shown here, Guy Gonzales, is renowned in his own right for autobiographical art about "living the life back then in the day."

Al Goldstein put out magazines that put out

Gay

X

Smut

Death magazine

Gadget

Cigar

Mobster Times

SCREW West

National SCREW

Best of SCREW

Bitch

Sex Sense

Homo/Ramrod

Code Words and Looks

Two women on the cover of a 1962
pocket paperback — one woman dreamily
looking at another — always meant
lesbian content. These mass-market
books, first popularized during World
War II, were meant to appeal to men,
but closeted lesbians picked up on the
codes that set these books apart from
other lurid titles on drugstore racks.
21 Gay Street in Greenwich Village was
where, in real life, "live and let live"
prevailed at a time when the Village
was a hotbed of bohemian and gay life.

21 GAY STREET

By SHELDON LORD
(an original novel)

40¢
MIDWOOD

NO. Y159

**GREENWICH VILLAGE, WHERE ANGELS
AND ADDICTS, LOVERS AND LESBIANS,
BOHEMIANS AND BAWDS LIVE AND LOVE**

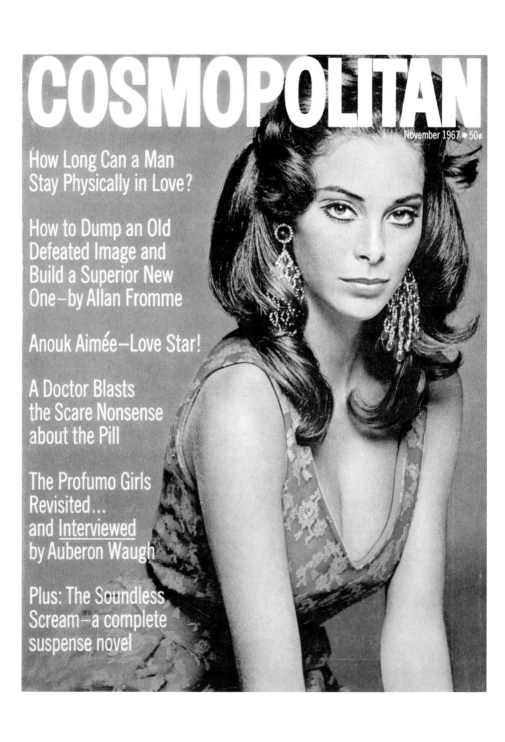

COSMOPOLITAN

November 1967 ● 50¢

How Long Can a Man
Stay Physically in Love?

How to Dump an Old
Defeated Image and
Build a Superior New
One—by Allan Fromme

Anouk Aimée—Love Star!

A Doctor Blasts
the Scare Nonsense
about the Pill

The Profumo Girls
Revisited...
and Interviewed
by Auberon Waugh

Plus: The Soundless
Scream—a complete
suspense novel

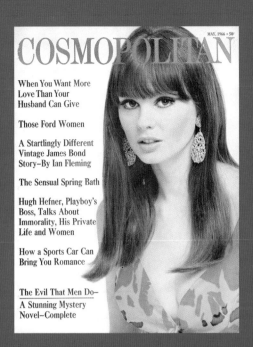

COSMOPOLITAN

MAY, 1966 • 50¢

When You Want More
Love Than Your
Husband Can Give

Those Ford Women

A Startlingly Different
Vintage James Bond
Story—By Ian Fleming

The Sensual Spring Bath

Hugh Hefner, Playboy's
Boss, Talks About
Immorality, His Private
Life and Women

How a Sports Car Can
Bring You Romance

The Evil That Men Do—
A Stunning Mystery
Novel—Complete

COSMOPOLITAN

November, 1966 • 50¢

The Fidelity Test—to
Tell if He's Cheating

Jacqueline Kennedy
Comes off Her Pedestal

Marry a Man Not Your
Equal—and Relax

How Close Are You to a
Nervous Breakdown?

Françoise Sagan's Latest
(Possibly Best) Novel

A New Mystery
By John D.
MacDonald

The
Complete
Bra Chart
(See Page 112)

The *Cosmo* Girl

Helen Gurley Brown's 1962 bestseller, *Sex and the Single Girl*, was a manifesto of the independent career woman. In 1965 the Arkansas-born Brown became editor of the old *Cosmopolitan* magazine and made it an international sensation. The *Cosmo* Girl loved men, sex, and beauty as well as her job. *Cosmo*'s daring, glamourous photography brought European sexual sophistication to American women's magazines. In 1972 it featured the first-ever nude male centerfold. Often attacked by male-bashing early feminists, Brown was in fact a prophetic precursor of the pro-sex feminism of the 1990s.

Bra-zen Acts

Don't blame men. In 1922 Ida Rosenthal
and Enid Bissett, partners in Enid Frocks
on West Fifty-seventh Street, protested
the in-vogue flat-chested look by creating
a garment to support the bust's natural
contours: the "Maidenform." At first,
their aim was purely practical — the bra
had to provide lift and shape. But comfort
and flexibility went hand in hand with
midcentury working women's growing
autonomy. The company's "Dream"
campaign, which ran from 1949 to 1969,
revolutionized intimate-apparel
advertising by featuring women in their
bras acting out fantasies of independence
in public places. In a breathtaking spot
from 1962, the dream of independence
practically borders on the insane.

COSTUME BY BETTY HETZ

I dreamed I walked a tightrope
in my *maidenform bra*

Sweet Music*...new Maidenform bra...has fitted **elastic** band under the cups for **easy** breathing;
and reinforced undercups to **keep** you at your peak of prettiness! White in A, B, C cups, 2.50

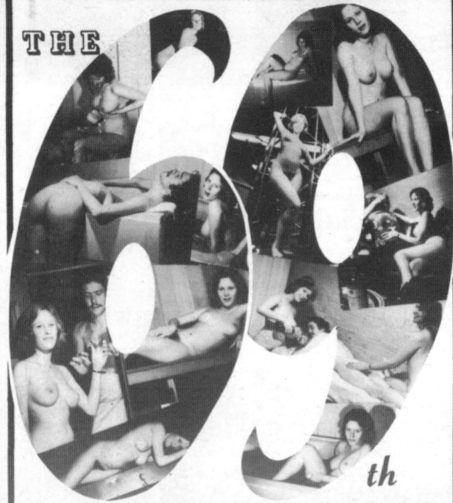

Relax and Release

Newly returned Vietnam vets, who got used to special treatments by Asian women while on duty in the 1960s and 70s, made the massage parlor business boom in New York. Still legal (prostitution is not), massage parlors offer stressed-out males the chance to turn to jelly and then get hard again. The massage is paid for up front, with the fee going to management, and then the masseuse negotiates her tip as the customer is enjoying a shiatsu or Swedish workover. Her tip depends on whether the usual manual release is performed topless or nude. More extensive services are available at a higher price. Who wouldn't want to cut right to the good stuff with some smashing 70s "coffee, tea or me" vixens?

The Great Pubic Wars

In the mid-1960s the Brooklyn-born artist and *Playboy* enthusiast Robert Charles Edward Sabatini Guccione decided that he could do a better job. While in London selling mail-order pinups, he shot his own first spread, launching a more explicit girlie mag. (Bob also captured the one opposite.) In February 1970 *Penthouse* presented the first glimpse of pubic hair in the mainstream media, and a year later the magazine went further with a full frontal-nude centerfold. Nervous *Playboy* followed with one of its own in 1972, launching a pitched battle in the pubic wars.

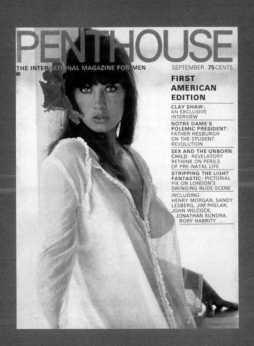

Media King and Queen

New York–bred media royalty — the shock-jock Howard Stern and "New York's best-kept secret," Robin Byrd — have kept radio and TV full of sex for a quarter century. Byrd, a fine arts college graduate, adult film star (remember her part in *Debbie Does Dallas* in 1976?), nude dancer, and cable porn show producer and hostess since 1979, pioneered adult programming on cable TV. She and Al Goldstein *(Screw)* and Lou Maletta of Gay Cable

News challenged Time Warner Cable and won a U.S. Supreme Court ruling giving them the right to run their porn shows on their local cable system. Stern, the self-proclaimed "King of all Media," offers the public a little sex in the morning on his drive-time radio show. The most fined man in the history of the Federal Communications Commission, he continues to serve up raunchy, politically incorrect programming because people listen.

Traffic Stoppers

No one living in or visiting New York can miss its traffic-stopping displays of sex and sensuality in the flesh or on advertising posters and billboards. Calvin "Nothing comes between me and my Calvins" Klein was the first fashion designer to use the buff male body to target gay men. His 1984 men's underwear campaign, which made women drool too, featured the aloof bronzed beauty Tom Hinthaus (left). Klein's steamy, in-your-face style was replicated in the giant billboards and bus posters advertising *Sex and the City,* HBO's award-winning adult comedy TV show about four sexually liberated career women in Manhattan—today's "It" girls. Witty Kim Cattrall (opposite), who plays the show's glamorous sex bomb, Samantha, has written a book with her husband, Mark Levinson, entitled *Satisfaction: The Art of the Female Orgasm* (Warner Books, 2002).

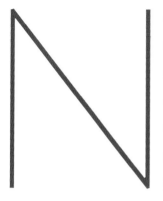

New York is synonymous with entertainment, and its residents are passionate about theater and cinema, sometimes to the point of rioting. The split between the working-class and the uptown theatrical worlds became evident when the Bowery Theater (1826) on the East Side, known for its coarse performances, rivaled the refined, Anglophilic Broadway. Radical artists and performers have taken their sometimes sexual statements off-Broadway, off-off-Broadway, and, when all else fails, into the streets. Beginning years of provocative, experimental films made in and about the city, early filmmakers focused on love, romance — and sex. Even Thomas A. Edison knew what sold: his 1896 film *The Kiss,* a reenactment of a scene from Broadway's *The Widow Jones* (1895), shocked audiences. And in the 1970s and 80s Grace Jones exploded onto the New York scene with her disco hits and cutting-edge performance art. What dancer Josephine Baker was to Paris in the 1920s, Jones was to New York a half century later — a new-wave icon of liberated female sexuality. Born in Jamaica, she was the first singer to perform live at Studio 54 and later became a fashion model, an actress, and a music-video pioneer. Jones's stage personae were futuristic, primitive, or androgynous (as when she sported a crew cut with a man's business suit). She played S&M robots, sexy animals, and tribal priestesses. In a 1985 performance at Paradise Garage, Jones collaborated with the painter Keith Haring to transform herself into a stylized queen of the urban jungle. David Spada turned her breasts into stiff, phallic cones recalling an Alexander Calder sculpture of — who else? — Josephine Baker. ♥

In the Flesh

Stage hits on lower Broadway helped ease the pain of the Civil War. *Mazeppa* (left), an equestrian blood-and-thunder drama based on a Lord Byron epic, starred Adah Isaacs Menken (1835–68), the sensation of the Victorian age. Menken was called "The Naked Lady" and the "most perfectly developed woman in the world" when she played the role of a Cossack prince who was stripped naked by a troop of soldiers, tied to a wild horse,

and sent galloping to his death. In 1866 America's first real musical extravaganza, *The Black Crook* (right) at Niblo's Garden included a stranded Parisian ballet corps and America's first can-can among its stunning effects. Who cared about the scenery when there was a bevy of ballerinas in flesh-colored tights doing a March of the Amazons in a moonlit grotto? Flesh-pink tights came in handy in both shows.

Twenty-three Skidoo

On one stretch of Twenty-third Street, a hot-air shaft would blow women's dresses up to indecent levels for the day. Newsboys, bootjacks, and other men on the street merely got a thrill, but Thomas A. Edison (1847–1931) actually captured the action in 1901 to make one of the first titillating films. Around the same time, a huge updraft was created when Daniel H. Burnham's Flatiron Building was completed in 1903 at the intersection of Twenty-third and Fifth Avenue. The result was an effect similar to the man-made air gust, followed by more naughty voyeurism. Men (those who weren't afraid that the building would fall on them) hung out around the corner to catch a glimpse of an ankle. To shoo gawkers from the area, cops on duty yelled "Twenty-three skidoo."

"I'm Not Gay. I Just Like Pearls"

As strict Victorian sex and gender conventions loosened, female impersonators were free to camp it up. Julian Eltinge (1883–1941), born Bill Dalton, was the top drag performer of the day in vaudeville, on Broadway, and in Hollywood. Eltinge, who ran around with stage and screen royalty, respected women — he tastefully emulated the most fashionable ladies, Gibson Girls, and bathing beauties. Although Eltinge endorsed women's beauty products, he kept his off-stage image manly by boxing and fighting gangsters. Rumors have it that he was romantically involved with a number of prominent men, including Rudolph Valentino, with whom he starred in *An Adventuress* (1916). Eltinge is thought to have been the "Lady in Black," the annual visitor to Valentino's grave. A theater on Forty-second Street was named after him.

Dirty Dancing

Isadora Duncan (1877–1927) (seen above in 1916) thought that ballet deformed women's bodies. Believing that the dance of the future would be based on freedom and naturalness, as it was with the ancient Greeks, she studied Delsarte techniques (the science of movement) and burlesque skirt dancing, in which the body is revealed through undulating diaphanous skirt fabric. Ruth St. Denis (1878–1968), who hit Manhattan in 1892, about six years before Duncan, also did skirt dancing in vaudeville and dime museums and later gave private lessons to Gertrude Vanderbilt Whitney. She was interested in Eastern cultures, incorporating exotic Indian, Egyptian, and Japanese customs into her dancing. In 1914 she teamed with the tango and ragtime dancer Ted Shawn (1891–1972) (opposite) for more reasons than one. Soon Martha Graham (1894–1991), a student of the Denishawn Company, would give audiences a rise with her sexual, thrusting dance motions.

Taming the Animal

The beginning of the twentieth century was the beginning of a new social age heralding all sorts of unbridled, mixed-race, and mixed-sex leisure activities such as dancing. The dance craze of the 1910s went hand in hand with ragtime music, whose roots lay in the black community. At the center of the cultural storm was the husband-and-wife dance team of Irene and Vernon Castle. The old order held that the "animal" dances of the day — the Bunny Hop, Turkey Trot, and Grizzly Bear, which got people off their seats and shaking, wig-

gling, and touching more than ever before — were obscene. Irene and Vern conveyed elegance and respectability to modern ballroom dancing, keeping breast-to-chest positions, and set trends in both dance and fashion. The duo is famous for the Castle Walk, a version of the brisk one-step.

"Between Two Evils, I Always Pick the One I Never Tried Before"

Vaudeville's "baby vamp" developed her saucy persona in melodramas such as her 1926 play *Sex,* about a Montreal prostitute. It packed houses until she was charged with lewd behavior. The Brooklyn-born Blonde Bombshell did ten days in jail and then rewrote her homosexual play, *The Drag,* as *The Pleasure Man*, featuring a heterosexual lead, but that too was raided. The gal with forty-three-inch assets next made the smash hit *Diamond Lil* (1928), tracing a saloon hostess who gets tangles with escaped convicts and white slaves. In the 1930s her wink-wink sexuality made Mae West (1893–1980) one of Hollywood's biggest stars.

Black Venus

Josephine Baker (1906–75) made her
mark on Manhattan but found success
abroad, in France, where this black Venus
was a sensation beginning in 1925. Known
mostly for her unconventional, exotic
performances — in Paris she danced the
Charleston wearing only a girdle of feathers
or with only a string of bananas around her
waist — she was one of the first black
performers to appeal to mixed audiences.
She herself had lovers of both sexes.
Baker's jazz-inspired performances, such
as this one from 1936, were always an
energetic mix of sensuality and comedy.
Although she starred in the Ziegfeld Follies
the same year, after achieving fame abroad,
her newly refined, sophisticated act seemed
uppity to New Yorkers. Twenty-seven
years later, slow-to-catch-on Americans
finally gave Baker a well-deserved standing
ovation at Carnegie Hall in 1973.

All God's Chillun'

All God's Chillun' Got Wings, a dignified black drama by Eugene O'Neill (1888–1953), opened at the Provincetown Playhouse in the Village in 1924 to outrage and criticism from the press. The play starred Paul Robeson, an African American lawyer-turned-actor, and Mary Blair, a white actress, in the roles of husband and wife. They received vicious hate mail, and a *New York Times* critic suggested that the play's implied miscegenation threatened the very blood of America. For this drama O'Neill, who wrote three plays with black casts, received a death threat on his son from the Ku Klux Klan. The playwright, later a Nobel Prize winner, sent a letter in large lettering back to the KKK member in Georgia: "Go fuck yourself!"

Lulu

With her famous black-helmet hair and
sexy showgirl lifestyle, Louise Brooks
(1906–85) — the quintessential flapper —
was a fine dancer, actress, and writer. After
dancing with Denishawn and appearing in
the George White Scandals and Ziegfeld
Follies in 1925, the radiant, smart, and sexy
Brooks went on to Paramount, starring in
flapper roles like *Love 'Em and Leave 'Em*
(1926) and *Rolled Stockings* (1927). A focal
point of the Jazz Age cult of youth, she
socialized with glamorous and artistic
figures of the 1920s, among them George
Gershwin and F. Scott Fitzgerald, and she
inspired the flapper cartoon *Dixie Dugan*.
Her most memorable performances were
as the sublimely erotic Lulu in G. W. Pabst's
Diary of a Lost Girl (1926) and his German
classic *Pandora's Box* (1929). Like other
flappers, she was known to coyly bare all
for the camera from time to time.

"It" Girls

The Brooklyn-born Clara Bow (1906–65) (second from left) had "it" in the 1927 movie based on Elinor Glyn's novel about a person who had a "purely virile quality." Dealing with infatuation, love among different classes, and single motherhood, it was the classic flapper movie. Max Fleischer, the leader of New York–style animation, created Betty Boop at the end of the Roaring Twenties. Modeled on the singer Helen Kane, Betty began as a dog girlfriend of Bimbo. Soon she stole the show and became human, with a strapless red dress that often got lost and sassy flirtations — males would even cop a boop-oop-de-doop feel. The fun (Hays Code) police came in 1934, turning the jazzy Miss Boop into boring Betty.

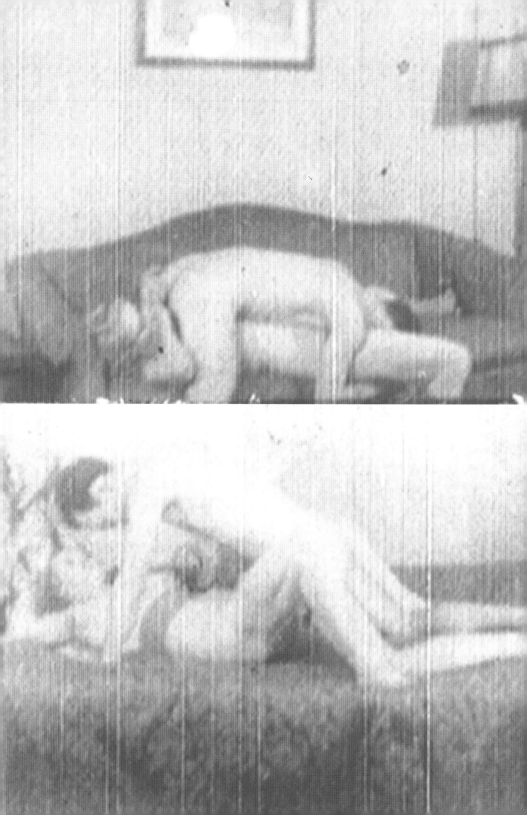

Gigolette

In *Gigolette,* a stag film made around 1931, a gal and her dog Lappy go walking across the new George Washington Bridge, encountering Tom, Dick, and Harry along the way. She takes them back to her apartment, where she lets just one in for a whopping good time. These illegal, titillating, primitive films (also known as smokers, blue movies, and cooch reels) were first made available sometime between 1915 and 1923 by traveling projectionists, who furtively showed backroom flicks, produced underground and managed by the mob, through thick cigar smoke at male bonding sessions. If moralists found the films, the cache would be destroyed and the vendor might be jailed. Playful nudies or explicit stag films always had simple plots and amateur actors, with nothing to hide; lacking Hollywood slickness, smokers actually had a very appealing realism. Shown in black and white, they were usually degraded

after generations of duping. After the late 1960s, softcore and hardcore films in theaters took their place.

A Dress Only Marilyn Would Wear

The Dress — the full-length, flesh-colored, sheer soufflé gauze "second skin" with six thousand rhinestones and sequins, designed by Jean Louis — was so perfectly fit that Marilyn Monroe (1926–62) had to be sewn into it the night she sang "Happy Birthday" to President John F. Kennedy. Adlai Stevenson, who attended the May 19, 1962, Democratic fundraiser and party for JFK, called the sight of Marilyn "skin and beads." Madison Square Garden was packed for what would be the sex goddess's last public performance. Peter Lawford kept the crowd entertained until Marilyn, notoriously late, finally made her entrance. When she appeared onstage with tussled hair (a wig), rumors flew. The star was tentative but went on to seduce the audience with her breathy nightclub-style rendition of "Happy Birthday." "I can now retire from politics," remarked the president, "after having had 'Happy Birthday' sung to me in such a sweet, wholesome way." The gown was left to Marilyn's mentor, the acting coach Lee Strasberg. In 1999 this perfect outfit, which originally cost $12,000, was sold at Christie's for $1.2 million.

*Some other mainstream films about
New York that packed theaters:*

King Kong (1933)

*Beauty and the Beast meet in the
ultimate urban jungle — New York.
Premiered at Radio City Music Hall.*

Butterfield 8 (1960)

*A high-class prostitute (Liz Taylor) tells
her married lover: "Not for sale."*

The Boys in the Band (1970)

*Gay men play painful outing games in a
first major studio look at homosexuality.*

Shaft (1971)

*"Who's the black private dick that's
a sex machine for all the chicks? Shaft!"*

Klute (1971)

*A call girl (Jane Fonda) looks for her
big acting break in New York.*

Saturday Night Fever (1977)

*A paint-store clerk (John Travolta) becomes
king of the local dance floor at night.*

Looking for Mr. Goodbar (1977)

*A Catholic teacher of the deaf becomes a
sexually adventurous bar cruiser by night.*

Cruising (1980)

*An undercover cop gets twisted
in an alien gay S&M world*

Celluloid Sex

A list of films made in or about New York
with overt or underlying sexual themes
might stretch around all of Times Square.
Midnight Cowboy (1969) (opposite) was the
first X-rated film to win an Oscar (1969).
This end-of-the-Swinging Sixties,
ultrarealistic tale follows a pretty-boy
dishwasher, Joe Buck (Jon Voight), as he
heads to New York to be a fantasy cowboy
gigolo. Although his first trick is with a
prostitute (Sylvia Miles) who takes him for
every cent he has, Buck goes on to find a
real one (Brenda Vaccaro, shown opposite
with Voight) at a Warhol-style party. He
then turns a homosexual trick to make
money to send his sickly pal, "Ratso"
(Dustin Hoffman), to Miami. The lurid,
personal subject matter that got *Cowboy*
the new X rating (including a suggested
blow job) generally shocked audiences.

Flaming Creatures

Directors such as Federico Fellini and John Waters were inspired by the films of Jack Smith, who – along with Kenneth Anger, Gregory Markopolous, and Andy Warhol – was one of the most influential avant-garde downtown filmmakers. Smith's innovative *Flaming Creatures* opened in 1961 to raids, arrests, and confiscation. Censored as pornography, the film is an almost cubist look at the human body, with shifting abstractions of penises, nipples, feet, and lips, all presented on ethereal stolen army surplus film, sometimes seen through layers of fabric. Paying homage to Hollywood B movies, *Flaming Creatures* is a campy, bizarre, creepy tale of orgies, vampires, and transvestites in agony, ecstasy, and general pandemonium.

Trash

Drug addicts do anything for a fix in *Trash* (1970), for which Paul Morrissey (fresh from playing in *Midnight Cowboy*) served as writer, director, and cinematographer. Morrissey's cinema verité picture uses real-life drug addicts, prostitutes, and homeless people to paint a grittier, more realistic picture. But the streetwise Joe Dallesandro, Holly Woodlawn, and others are indeed acting, even though they used their real first names in the film. No Hollywood actors could have gotten this close to their subjects, and no Hollywood director would have thought to use a transvestite (Holly) for realism in 1970. Holly searches the city's trash for goodies, and Joe tries to hustle heroin off a variety of women, including Holly's pregnant sister, but his impotence gets in the way. Joe and Holly come up with a brilliant plan to try to adopt a baby to get on welfare.

Skindependent Exploitation

Known as the "Queen of Nudies" for her 1960s low- to no-budget "Ninth Avenue" exploitation films, the native New Yorker Doris Wishman shows sympathy for her own gender's tough world. Like all sexploitation films, sex is alluded to, but genital action was never allowed. Before her softcore porn, she made a "roughie," equating sex with violence, called *Bad Girls Go to Hell* (1965) (above). In it a housewife (Gigi Darlene) kills a rapist, gets beaten by a sadist, is raped by a married man, and is propositioned by a lesbian. Wishman's major effort of the 1970s was to harness the talent of Chesty "Zsa Zsa" Morgan (opposite). Chesty and her 73-inch bust starred in *Deadly Weapons* (1973), giving her an opportunity to smother assassins with her colossal breasts, and in *Double Agent 73* (1974), which has her snapping drug dealers' pictures by removing her tentlike brassiere and pressing a button in her boob. *Each Time I Kill* premiered in 2002.

216

Greek Glory

Who'd have thought that the biggest wig of the Times Square porn film industry was a Greek lesbian with two girlfriends? Chelly Wilson gave her theaters Hellenic names like Venus, Adonis, and Eros. Her Avon films, from softcore to gay hardcore, were some of the roughest extra-low-budget films around and starred Vanessa Del Rio, Sharon Mitchell, Ambrosia Fox, Jamie Gillis, Marc Stevens, George Payne, Velvet Summers, Cheri Champagne, Nico, and Annie Sprinkle. Big directors were Joe Davian and Phil Prince.

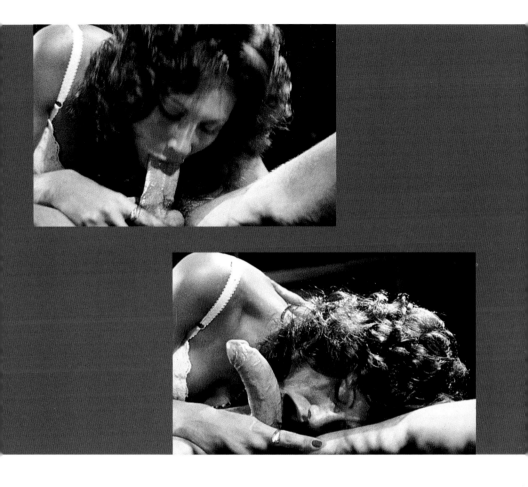

Deep Inside Porn

Deep Throat (1972) made hardcore porn fashionable. Directed by Gerard Damiano and starring Linda Lovelace and Harry Reems, it demonstrated the intricacies of fellatio for hip middle-class women who had never been in a porn theater before. The film reportedly grossed $600 million, but Lovelace — backed by feminists — later claimed that she was paid nothing and that her husband, Chuck Traynor, had forced her to do it. The film entered American history by lending its name to a key Watergate informer.

Meatjoy

Using raw fish, chickens, sausages, paint, rope, and more, the multidisciplinary artist Carolee Schneemann brought *Meatjoy* to the Judson Church Theater in Greenwich Village in 1964. She called it a "propulsion toward the ecstatic — shifting and turning between tenderness, wilderness, precision, abandon: qualities which could at any moment be sensual, comic, joyous, repellent." In 1975 she gained notoriety for *Interior Scroll,* a performance in which she read from a paper scroll pulled from her vagina, the source of knowledge.

Seedbed

When he installed a urinal upside down (called *Fountain*, by R. Mutt) in a gallery in 1917, Marcel Duchamp led the way for artists to break the boundaries between public and private. In the 1960s and 70s the International Fluxus movement and political happenings led artists to act out their issues in public, with humor and shocking realism. Vito Acconci, a poet and performance and installation artist, performed *Seedbed* at New York's Sonnabend Gallery in 1972. He spent hours on end lying under a ramp, voicing his sexual fantasies and masturbating while people walked over him.

Grunt and Grope Theater

New York was turned into a stage in the late 1960s and the 1970s for sociopolitical drama. Love-ins and other dramatic communal statements were enacted by the "do your own thing" generation. Action painting and happenings broke the boundaries of fine art and theater. Separation between actors and audiences was reduced to nothing. *Dionysus in 69* — based on Euripides's *Bacchae,* directed by Richard Schechner, and performed by the Performance Group at 33 Wooster Street — portrayed the full circle of time, bringing to life the patron of poetry, song, ritual dance, mysticism, and winemaking. The intuitive photographer Max Waldman shot this baroque drama in 1969. Theatergoers could not only watch nude, orgiastic scenes by young actors but also might be pulled on-stage for a good feel of their own.

Odd Jobs

Deborah Harry and Madonna Ciccone pulled some odd jobs in New York on their way to stardom. In the 1970s Debbie (opposite) was a Playboy bunny and waitressed at Max's Kansas City. Madonna (above) showed off her dancer's physique as an artist's and photographer's model.

Bathhouse Bette

The Continental Baths in the Ansonia Hotel's basement — including an Olympic-size swimming pool, disco dance floor, sauna rooms, and cabaret lounge — boasted that they revived "the glory days of ancient Rome." Opened by Steve Ostrow in the late 1960s, the gay bathhouse in the early 1970s put a struggling nightclub singer named Bette Midler on a roster of top entertainers along with Melba Moore and the Manhattan Transfer. The Divine Ms. M. wowed audiences with her "trash with flash" routines. She even got her shy pianist, Barry Manilow, to play in nothing but a towel (a uniform available at Bloomingdale's). Straight men and women streamed in to see her, but some gay guys obsessed with the steamy sex were peeved that she stole the show. By 1974 gays left when the acts got extremely campy, and then the baths went coed and were finally closed.

Real Dolls

When commercial success didn't hit the New York Dolls in the mid-1970s, Malcolm McLaren — soon to bring the Sex Pistols to fame — dressed his proto-punk band in red leather and had them play in front of a Soviet flag, betraying their communist sympathies. Record companies, which had already shied away from this cross-dressing, "vulgar" group, were even less inclined to sign it up. The group, including David Johansen, Johnny Thunders, Syl Sylvain, Arthur Kane, and Billy Murcia, had formed in 1971 and quickly developed a local following for their mix of hard (Stones) and glam (Bowie) rock, androgyny, and generally entertaining antics.

Freedom of Choice

Candida Royalle, president of Femme Productions, makes things that women enjoy: erotic films and stylish, ergonomic vibrators. The native New Yorker, with roots in the arts and music, headed to San Francisco in the 1970s to sing in jazz clubs and be a part of the avant-garde theater scene, even working with the John Waters character Divine. To earn extra money, she acted in twenty-five X-rated films, such as *Hot Rackets* (1979), *Ultra Flesh* (1981), and *Blue Magic* (1980) (above), her swan song, which she wrote. Directing and producing her own films in the 1980s (below), she emphasized foreplay, sensuality, and even the erotic use of condoms, a must for her. In 1984 *Urban Heat,* Femme's second movie (of fifteen), was full of hot summer sex in New York. Royalle's mail-order video business thrived, serving erotica to women who didn't want to go into skeevy theaters. A founding member of the New York–based Feminists for Free Expression, she takes an anticensorship stance when it comes to sex on screen.

Working Sex

Mainstream feminism in the 1970s and 80s called for a ban on pornography. Seeking common ground, feminists, sex workers, and performance artists — including Annie Sprinkle, Veronica Vera, and Candida Royalle — made a clean breast of it (left) in 1984 at the Second Coming, a New York conference sponsored by the pro-choice collective Carnival Knowledge that got the performance center Franklin Furnace in trouble with the NEA. Seamlessly blending sex worker and performance artist, Penny Arcade (below), a superstar at Warhol's Factory, explored sexual issues from prostitution to censorship in shows such as *Bitch! Dyke! Faghag! Whore!*

Dance for Survival

Throughout his career, Bill T. Jones used sexual themes in his dances to "hit people over the head" about sociopolitical issues. This African American dancer and choreographer from upstate New York met the Bronx-born, Jewish Arnie Zane at SUNY Binghamton and began collaborating in dance and love in 1971. They burst on the scene with highly provocative erotic dances that addressed racism, sexism, and homophobia, collaborating in the 1980s with artists and designers such as Robert Longo, Keith Haring, and Willi Smith. *Continuous Replay* (opposite), featuring Justice Allen, Jones, Arthur Aviles (concealed), and Andrea Smith and choreographed by Zane, was performed at P.S. 122 in 1991. After losing Zane to AIDS in 1988, Jones, himself HIV positive, premiered *Still/Here* (1994), a dance about survival, at the Brooklyn Academy of Music. Arlene Croce of the *New Yorker* called it "victim art," setting off a controversy over the fine line between art and sexual politics. In the late 1990s, shedding the overt politics and narratives, Jones took his dance troupe back to the roots of dance and sexuality to focus solely on movement.

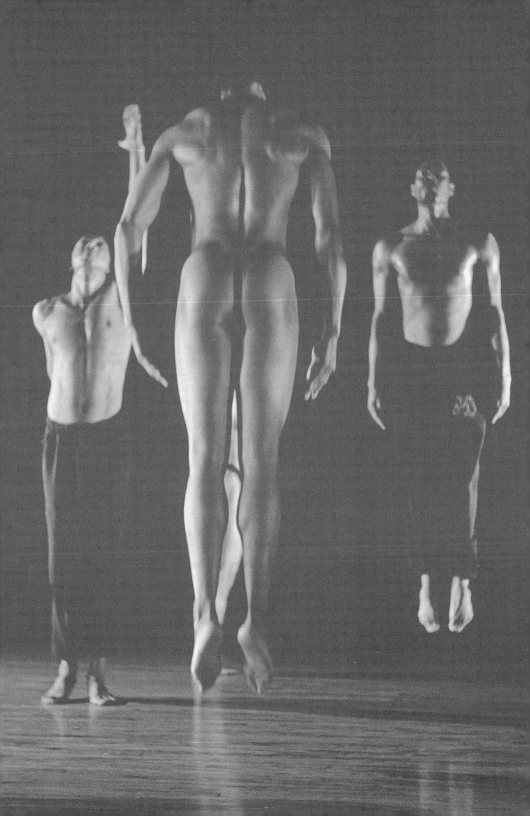

She's Gotta Have It

The breakthrough film for the Brooklyn-based Spike Lee, an NYU Tisch School graduate, *She's Gotta Have It* (1986) features a talented, independent young woman, Nola Darling (Tracy Camilla Johns) trying to have noncommittal relationships with three very different men. The film's beautifully done sex scenes depend on the unique characters of Nola's men. One boyfriend is an egotistical male model with a great body, while Spike Lee himself sets out the other extreme, a funky bike messenger named Mars Blackmon. Another is right in the middle, but all want her for their own. This low-budget film, which was shot by David Lee and won the Prix de Jeunesse at the Cannes Film Festival (1986), helped propel the American independent film movement of the 1980s.

The Voluptuous Horror of Karen Black

Karen Black, the star of 1970s flicks like *Easy Rider, Five Easy Pieces,* and the cult classic horror tale *Trilogy of Terror*, just may be the only actress with a rock band named after her. Shows by the goth rock band called the Voluptuous Horror of Karen Black reach the level of performance art. Combining burlesque, vaudeville, and bizarro films, the group regularly includes frontal nudity and raunchy acts. Breaking eggs full of paint on the lead's vagina is typical. This non-drug-using band — featuring the vocalist Kembra Pfahler, the guitarist Samoa, and a bevy of dancers — does songs such as "Rabid Bikini Model" and "Underwear Drawer," in which a chest of drawers is dragged on-stage full of underwear that is thrown out into the audience. A photograph in *The Anti-Naturalists* (1995), one of the group's CDs, shows Pfahler's vagina sewed shut.

Metamorphosexual

No aspect of sex or the human body escapes the attention of Dr. Annie Sprinkle (opposite), shown doing her "sex magic" masturbation ritual, the Legend of the Ancient Sacred Prostitute, in her 1990 show *Post Porn Modernist*. A newly minted doctor of sexology, this multitalented, multimedia sex artist began her career as a model, prostitute, and star of more than 150 porn films, ending up an acclaimed writer, director, teacher, photographer, activist, and performance artist. New York has been the perfect incubator for performances such as a "Liberty Love Boat" trip to the Statue of Liberty to protest

Mayor Rudolph Giuliani's 1998 crackdown on the city's sex industry. At the Sprinkle Salon on Lexington Avenue, Sprinkle photographed another New York–spawned Renaissance woman, the confrontational Lydia Lunch (left), whose work ranges from sex and violence films to music and poetry. Knowing no taboos, she simply gives in to her predatory masculine tendencies and lets loose her darker desires, challenging audiences to prove that "pain, torture and sexual deviousness are universal traits."

Hard Core

Countless sexually explicit hip-hop artists have come out of the New York region, from LL Cool J to Puff Daddy. But Lil' Kim, from Bedford Stuyvesant, rivals her brothers with some seriously sexually assertive lyrics, edgy rhythms, and hot poses. Lil' Kim models her fashions after Marilyn Monroe and Tina Turner and other provocative black women enter-tainers. Mentored by Notorious B.I.G. and a part of the Junior M.A.F.I A. group, her first solo album *Hard Core* (1996), with tracks like "**** You" and "Queen B@$#h," put her at number 11 on the *Billboard* Top 200. At the MTV Music Awards in 1999, Diana Ross tweaked Lil' Kim's exposed pastie-covered nipple in front of the world.

CULTURE SHOCKING

To challenge the best European artists, New Yorkers continually push the envelope in terms of artistic form and content. After the turn of the twentieth century, many avant-garde artists moved to Manhattan from abroad (they continue to do so), knowing that it is the place for bold new artistic and intellectual statements. Of course, not everyone in New York is open to new and provocative ideas: western Europe has generally been much more liberated, especially when it comes to sexuality and representations of the nude (Italy and Spain especially have great traditions of nudity and ecstasy in religious art). Even as recently as 1999, Mayor Rudolph Giuliani almost sent the Brooklyn Museum of Art packing for, among other things, displaying a painting of Christ's last supper that features Jesus as a naked black woman (he deemed it "outrageous and disgusting"). Yet countless artists and designers who work with sexual themes or cater to sexual tastes don't raise much of an eyebrow in New York. The Baroness, for one, has made an art form out of latex. Although her ultrasensual material has fetishistic connotations, this artist has outfitted people heading to the opera and nightclubs or just to go shopping. The use of color sets her clothes apart from the typically dark dungeon-perfect fetish costumes. Inspired by the 1940s film producer Busby Berkeley as well as her own work in film and on theater sets, the Baroness loves to produce exotic fashion shows and hold fetish retinue balls at local trend-setting clubs and beyond the Hudson. For her, latex is "the perfect antidote for excess conventionalism." ❤

PHOTOGRAPHER MARK MCQUEEN

Nudes and Prudes

Art controversies in New York didn't begin yesterday. In 1810 Adolph Ulrich Wertmuller's (1751–1811) painting *Danae and the Shower of Gold* (1787) caused a sensation when it went on view. Nudes, especially by Old Masters, were acceptable in Europe, but attitudes toward art in antebellum America were set by the prudish middle class. Critics condemned the painting as "the pollution of art which offends pure taste and the morality of art," yet New Yorkers continued to pay to see this suggestion of sexual intercourse; special days were set aside for ladies' private viewings. It was reported that "crowds of both sexes sit together for hours gazing upon these very nude figures with delight." They must have wanted to assert their cultural and aesthetic erudition.

Diana, the Hunted

Victorian moralists had a problem with the first permanent installation of a nude woman in America. In 1893 the nation was shocked to see the goddess *Diana,* designed by the chic New York sculptor Augustus Saint-Gaudens (1848–1907), installed atop the Giralda Tower of Stanford White's Madison Square Garden. J. P. Morgan, however, was pleased with a tomb recently designed for him by Saint-Gaudens and White. Because Morgan was also the Garden's largest shareholder, the powerful thirteen-foot-high statue (the original eighteen-foot version was out of proportion) stayed put on her perch, aiming her bow at Admiral David Farragut, another Saint-Gaudens–White collaboration, in Madison Square Park. Taken down in 1932, the statue is now at the Philadelphia Museum of Art.

Icy Reception

Paul Chabas's painting *September Morn* (1912) won the Medal of Honor at the Paris Salon but did not stir any real interest. He got the bright idea to send the work — whose figure's head was modeled on an American girl, Julie Phillips — to New York, where it was promptly exhibited in a gallery window. Out hunting for vice, Anthony Comstock told the dealer, "There's too little morn and too much maid. Take her out!" The manager refused, and soon the painting was a national sensation, pictured on postcards and novelty items. Chabas finally sold the painting in Russia. When *Morn* was offered to the Philadelphia Museum of Art, it was rejected as having no place in the history of modern art. The Metropolitan Museum of Art took it; today its own postcards remain big sellers.

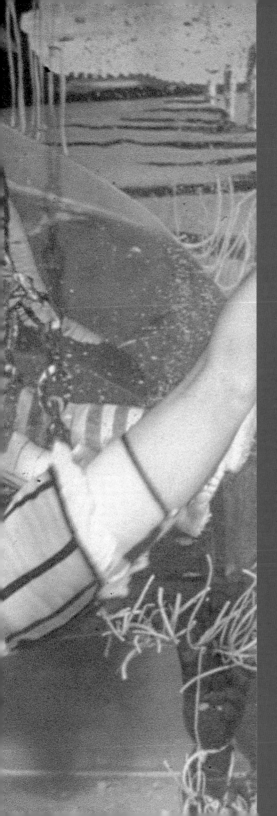

Man's Right to Love Women with Exotic Heads of Fish

Salvador Dali (1904–89), the European surrealist, arrived in the Cartesian city of Manhattan in the 1930s. After his lascivious mannequins were removed from a Bonwit Teller window, he completed his first architectural project at the 1939 World's Fair. Dubbed "20,000 Legs Under the Sea," Dali's building resembled exaggerated shellfish ornamented with plaster females and other oddities. Female divers in a tank practiced scales on a human piano. The sponsor, a rubber products maker, insisted that the "liquid ladies" wear rubber mermaid tails. Dali refused, and then retaliated with a manifesto on "man's right to love women with exotic heads of fish" and had an airplane drop copies of it over New York.

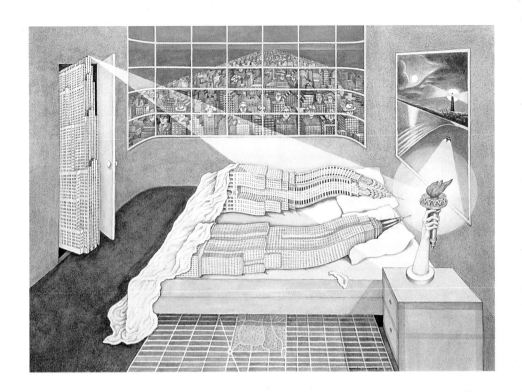

Anthropomorphous

Architecture with hormones? The French-born, longtime New York artist Louise Bourgeois made numerous works entitled *Femme Maison* ("housewife") (opposite) in the late 1940s, dehumanizing woman into a house and a domestic servant. Although some of them seem impenetrable, this one, with its broad stairway, is rather inviting. Other artists have taken the opposite approach and given architecture human qualities. Madelon Vriesendorp cofounded the Dutch Office for Metropolitan Architecture (OMA) with her husband, Rem Koolhaas. For his book *Delirious New York: A Retroactive Manifesto for Manhattan* (1978), Vriesendorp painted a postcoital scene in which the feminine Chrysler Building and the masculine Empire State Building are caught after the act by the humorless RCA Building (Anthony Comstock reincarnated?).

The Nifty Fifties

Bettie Page (opposite) was probably *the* pinup girl of the twentieth century, with her varied glamour, cheesecake, and bondage-and-discipline styles. The 36–23–35, dark-haired, beautiful once-poor girl from Tennessee moved to New York in the late 1940s and was soon noticed at Coney Island. Promptly introduced to the Camera Club scene – groups of amateur photographers whose favorite subject was cute, scantily clad girls in urban studios or suburban New York settings (above) – she went on to national exposure in the leading men's magazines. The artistic nude photographer Bunny Yeager photographed Page in 1955. From 1952 to 1957 Page worked with Irving Klaw and his sister, Paula, photographer-owners of the big *Movie Star News* (a photograph attributed to Klaw is below). She ushered in a new

B&D photo style, sporting corsets and other bondage gear but keeping it light. In the paranoid 1950s, it wasn't long before the Klaws were officially told to burn their negatives. Page left the business for good shortly after that, but since the 1990s a renewed cult interest in her has extended to the fashion industry. The legend kept her vow never to let her face be seen on camera or in print again.

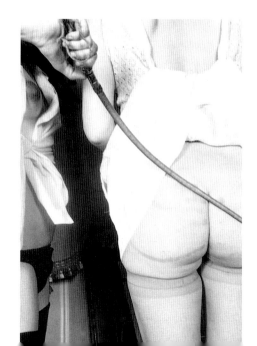

Bad Boy of American Literature

Brooklyn-born Henry Miller's (1891–1980) *Tropic of Cancer* (1934) used everyday language and taboo words — people *fucked,* and the *cunts* and *pricks* were described in detail. The characters in this tale of the ribald exploits of an expatriate writer in France were proud of their sexuality and their sexual organs. First published in France with the aid of Miller's lover, Anaïs Nin, it sold two million copies in two years, and GI's smuggled it into the States and Britain, where it was unpublishable. Barney Rossett of Grove Press took a chance and brought it out in 1961, selling 68,000 copies the first week. The U.S. Supreme Court finally gave its imprimatur in 1964, according Miller and *Tropic of Cancer* the status of fine art.

Dirty Words

The first modern comic — most 1950s comedians did strings of jokes and stories — Lenny Bruce (1925–66) offered social commentary, openly discussing sex and attacking racism and organized religion. A favorite in New York nightclubs in the early 1960s, he was arrested for obscenity four times between 1961 and 1964; the last time he dared to say *fuck* and *motherfucker* on stage at the Café au Go Go in Greenwich Village. After a hearing related to his pending trial, he left the federal courthouse on June 17, 1964, with his attorneys Ephraim London and Martin Garbus. Bruce wondered why it was okay to say the word *kill* in front of an audience, but when certain words for loving were uttered (as they were commonly used in society), one was hauled off to jail. Artists and celebrities from Woody Allen to Norman Mailer petitioned Mayor Robert Wagner to drop the charge, which restricted Bruce's constitutional right to free speech. Branded a "sick comic" and a "dirty comic," Bruce finally got a career-ending conviction in New York in 1964. It was overturned two years after his death of an alleged morphine overdose.

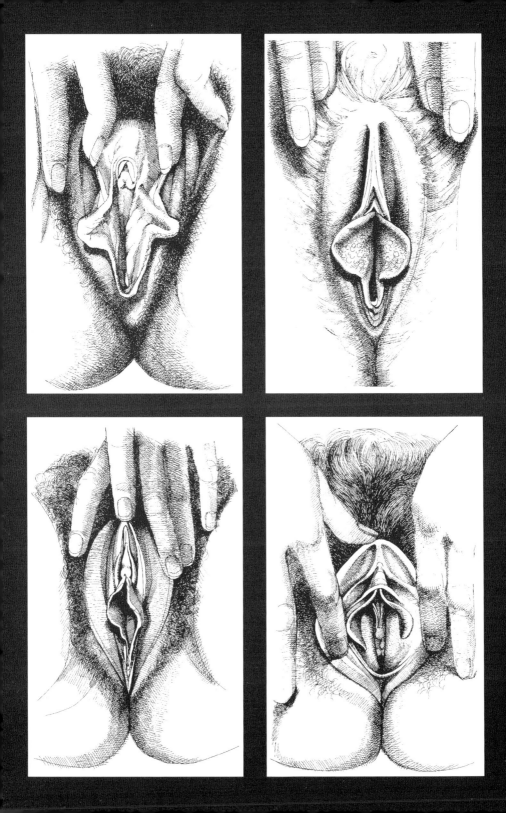

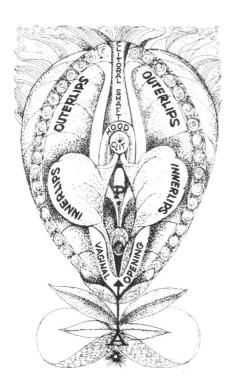

Viva la Vulva!

The artist Betty Dodson broke every barrier in her pioneering erotic art of the 1960s and 70s. As a therapist, Dodson has won renown for her promotion of sexual freedom: she is the liberator of masturbation and a celebrator of orgasms. Her body-sex workshops in New York inspired Eve Ensler's *Vagina Monologues* (1996). Dodson illustrated her *Liberating Masturbation: A Meditation on Self Love* (1974) with her own drawings (shown here). In 1988 the book was re-released as *Sex for One: The Joy of Selfloving.*

Pretty Baby

Brooke Shields took her first trip down the catwalk at age three and later starred in Louis Malle's *Pretty Baby* (1978) as Violet, a twelve-year-old prostitute. At ten, the Manhattan-born model-actress posed nude for the photographer Garry Gross. Six years afterward, she sued him to stop their publication but did not prevail. One of his images – copied by the appropriation artist Richard Prince and retitled *Spiritual America* – was shown at the Whitney Museum's *American Century* exhibition in 1999–2000 and sold at Christie's for $151,000 in 1999. But Gross did not receive credit or money for the sale. Unable to sue, he settled for $2,000 and his name added to any exhibition labels. The photograph shown here is his original.

New York Girls

A self-described hick transplanted from North Carolina, the photographer Richard Kern has always had a thing for New York girls (not necessarily born here). To him, they are twisted and tied sexpots, mischievous, tattooed, slutty, pasty, sexually adventurous, and know-and-like-what-they're-doing kind of gals. Living in Alphabet City, he finds some of his best models living just down the block, ready to go at a moment's notice. Kern is also known for his taboo-breaking, screaming "Cinema of Transgression" films with Nick Zedd, Lydia Lunch and Sonic Youth, David Wojanarowitcz, Karen Finley, and others.

D.C. Couldn't Take It

He shot beautiful flowers, vegetables, and celebrity portraits, but it was his graphic depictions of the 1970s underground gay male world, certain nudes, and children that catapulted an unknown artist from Long Island to stardom. Robert Mapplethorpe (1946–89) had his first big shows in 1977: flowers at the Holly Solomon Gallery and male nudes and sadomasochism at the Kitchen. The photographer's strict Catholic upbringing worked its way into his artwork as he developed his cool, classical style. His human figures — posed, cropped, and unyielding — seem as objectlike as his inanimate subjects seem human. Senator Jesse Helms and other conservatives attacked the National Endowment for the Arts for funding him and other sexually explicit artists (among them Andres Serrano, who showed a crucifix submerged in urine). Helms carried around with him Mapplethorpe's portrait of Rosie, a toddler with her crotch showing, as evidence. The Corcoran Gallery of Art in Washington sent Mapplethorpe's show, including his self-portrait with a bullwhip in his anus, packing to the nearby Washington Project for the Arts.

Tags

Marking territory with graffiti was on the rise in the 1960s (above) as a way for predominantly poor, inner-city young men to make the world know their names. Subway cars, themselves moving art galleries, offered an obvious canvas for their nicknames. Elaborate, sexy drawings often boosted the tags' viewership.

Flags

For folks who want a great ersatz-color dye job for their hair, the place to go is Patricia Field's glitter-glam boutique in Greenwich Village. The native New Yorker has achieved cult status for her Eighth Street shop and salon, a source over three decades for drag queens, nightlifers, and now the goth and industrial scene. Her House of Field includes a sexy clothing line by David Dalrymple, who created Britney Spears's provocative costume for the 2000 MTV Music Awards. A trendsetting, award-winning costume designer for TV and film, Field was the perfect pick to dress the chic cast of HBO's hit show *Sex and the City*.

Needle Art

In the late 1980s the photographer Charles Gatewood helped usher in the modern primitive movement, whose adherents express themselves erotically and artistically through tattoo, piercings, scarification, and other body modifications, bringing forbidden and antisocial art forms into the mainstream. Gatewood has followed, teamed with, and best-friended radical underground artists such as Annie Sprinkle, the erotic writer Marco Vassi, the Wood- stock poet and critic Michael Perkins, and Mam'selle Victoire, who all worked with the New York master tattoo artist Spider Webb and his Duchamp-inspired R. Mutt Press. Gatewood documented Webb's handiwork displayed live as well as on the walls of the Levitan Gallery in 1976.

PUBLIC DISPLAYS

P eople with a cause may go to Washington to tell the government, but when they want to tell the world, they head to New York. There is no bigger stage on which to publicly air grievances and expose injustices, and perhaps there is no more tolerant a place to do so. New York embraces politics of all kinds. Group parades, marches, protests, pickets, sit-ins, love-ins, and rallies over sexuality and sex rights and wrongs have been common throughout the Big Apple's history. But given the wealth of artists in the city, some political statements are bound to be made in a more creative or even devious way. Although New York has a state law against public nudity, a lot of ultra-buff guys and even some of the gals who march in the annual Lesbian, Gay, Bisexual, and Transgender Pride Parade like to test the police. A law prohibiting women from going topless was ruled unconstitutional in New York State and is essentially unenforceable. Other political battles over sex are constantly brewing in New York, some of them fought in the courts. In December 2001 the accomplished photographer Barbara Nitke – who photographs sexual situations from X-rated film sets to underground sex clubs and extraordinary extemporaneous sadomasochistic love scenes, such as *All Slaved Out* (1997) (opposite) – joined with the National Coalition for Sexual Freedom to oppose Internet censorship that would gag sexually explicit artists. "Community standards" in America's heartland, Nitke contends, shouldn't be allowed to stifle New York artists' freedom of expression and determine what New Yorkers access on their own computers. ❤

Fighting for Their Sex

In 1910 Fay Hubbard was one of an estimated fifty thousand members of the Woman Suffrage Party in New York. Energized by a younger generation, they lobbied, used civil disobedience, and went on hunger strikes to secure women's right to vote in national elections. For New York's first large suffrage parade that year, women donned all-white attire, carried banners, and marched in precision formation to show their resolve. Not everyone was pleased — both men and women called the suffragists names, complained about the presence of babies and children, and questioned the attendance figures. Seven years later New York State approved women's suffrage, and then, with passage of the Nineteenth Amendment to the U.S. Constitution in 1920, one battle of the sexes was won.

"Bunny Marie"

After Gloria Steinem moved to New York, she became a journalist and then a feminist activist. On her way up, she went undercover as a Playboy bunny for *Show* magazine in 1963. Other waitresses at the Playboy Club on East Fifty-ninth Street said that after a week, "Bunny Marie" went on leave with a trumped-up tale of family illness. In "A Bunny's Tale," Steinem portrayed Playboy bunnies as unhappy, naive, exploited victims – a description rejected by the talented bunnies, including Lauren Hutton and Kathryn Leigh Scott, who went on to successful careers.

Gloria's unofficial list of bunny bosom stuffers

*Kleenex · Plastic dry cleaning bags
Absorbent cotton · Cut-up bunny tails · Foam rubber
Lamb's wool · Kotex halves · Silk scarves*

Stonewalled

After midnight on June 27, 1969, when gays in New York
were still mourning the death of Judy Garland on June 22,
NYPD officers from the public morals section raided the
Stonewall Inn at 51–53 Christopher Street, near Sheridan
Square in Greenwich Village. Although they had been paid
off the week before, the police arrested employees on a
charge of serving alcohol without a license. Sympathetic
crowds gathered outside. After a woman dressed as a man
reportedly struggled with cops trying to get her into a
paddy wagon, drag queens and onlookers let loose, throwing bottles and even a Molotov cocktail.
Violent protests challenging the vice squad
harassment started the following two
nights, beginning a new era in gay liberation. The radical Gay Liberation Front and
Gay Activists Alliance were formed, and
those who remember the Stonewall now
march every year on the last Sunday of June.

© FRED W. McDARRAH

The Crusaders

Angry women also took to the streets of New York in the 1970s to protest sexual violence against women. Several incendiary books helped fuel the fire. Robin Morgan's *Theory and Practice: Pornography and Rape* (1974) described rape as any sex not initiated by women, and the Brooklyn-born Susan Brownmiller's *Against Our Will: Men, Women and Rape* (1975) claimed that rape is "a conscious process of intimidation" by which all men keep women in fear. With feminists demanding laws to protect women, while pornography was gaining greater legal protection, conflict was inevitable. Women Against Pornography rallies became common, and Take Back the Night marches featured testimony from rape victims.

If the medium is the message . . .

. . . don't get hit by it. In 1989 Gran Fury, a New York art collective spun off from the radical activist group ACT-UP, used city streets and transport as its canvas for art about the AIDS crisis. Alluring advertising merged with education and art.

REED AND INDIFFERENCE DO.

Glennda and Camille Downtown

Drag queens, porn stores, pick-up spots, and the Stonewall Inn are celebrated by
Camille Paglia and Glennda Orgasm (Glenn Belverio) in *Glennda and Camille Do Downtown*
(1993), a video shot in Greenwich Village for *Glennda and Friends,* Belverio's show on
Manhattan Cable Public Access Television. The two, seen here in front of a Betty Grable
cutout on Eighth Street, also tangle with antiporn feminist demonstrators. Rejected for
political incorrectness by the New York Lesbian and Gay Film Festival, the film won first
prize for best short documentary at the 1994 Chicago Underground Film Festival.

Suite Hearts Uptown

Cracking down on sex businesses and curbing risqué art in public institutions,
Mayor Rudolph Giuliani was one of the biggest keepers of public propriety.
However, in June 2001 the New York Post alleged that, while married to Donna
Hanover, Hizzoner and an Upper East Side single mom, Judith Nathan, were using a
St. Regis Hotel suite as a love nest — one more reason to drop out of the 2000
Senate race. Although he tried to sweep sexual expression under the carpet around
the city, he let his hang out in front of millions of people on New Year's Eve 2001.

It's Not the Easter Parade

What started as a two thousand-person march from Waverly Place in 1970 to commemorate the Stonewall rebellion a year earlier has turned into an annual gay parade each June that attracts 250,000 marchers and 350,000 spectators, a rally, the Pridefest outdoor party, and a waterfront dance, bringing millions of dollars to the city. Although it is a serious march for rights, the Mardi Gras–like party atmosphere of the Lesbian, Gay, Bisexual, and Transgender Pride event works to win over crowds. Since 1992, on the Saturday beforehand, lesbians have held their own Dyke March to combat discrimination. Less fantastic than the bigger march, it's a sight to see so many boobs bouncing down Fifth Avenue.

SCENES

The city is an incubator of scenes — infinite scenarios for all proclivities from unique happenings to regularly scheduled events and permanent hot spots. The most intense and publicity intensive always seem to incorporate sex, drugs, alcohol, avant-garde art, theater, fashion, unconventional music, or celebrities. Combine them all and an explosion results. In New York's early days, scenes were generated around taverns and theaters, usually segregated by race, sex, or class. In the nineteenth century, residents and visitors gravitated to entertainment venues and hit the sex districts, while the elite classes created highly restricted social gatherings. With the rise of cabarets in the twentieth century, classes and sexes mixed, and modern art, literature, and music spawned all kinds of morally relaxed bohemian scenes. Certain personalities, from Emma Goldman to Edna St. Vincent Millay, emerged as leaders of the pack from 1890 through the 1920s. With the proliferation of mass media in the 1960s, selling cool lifestyles and everything new, the most provocative creative types came together to push social limits. Pop music's special effects drove New York's orgiastic scene for both straights and gays. Scene impresarios became bigger than life. A 1960s Glitter Ball held at a New York disco was recorded by the photographer Charles Gatewood, a poet of the underground. The gala may have been inspired by Andy Warhol's silver-covered Factory, created by the artist's hairdresser-lighting man, who covered the studio pipes with silver foil and painted appliances the same. Pre–Studio 54 partygoers here carried drug use and self-indulgence into the Me Decade of the 1970s. ❤

Jitterbugging at the Savoy

Harlem's Savoy Ballroom, the most famous swing club in New York in the 1930s and 40s, was the place to be to be for wild and sweaty dancing to some of the hippest music of the day. Count Basie, a Savoy regular, was known for his more moderate beats, while Chick Webb put out tunes with whiplash tempos, perfect for jitterbuggers. Generally considered naughty and annoying – out-of-control dancers disrupted musicians by shouting out requests, clapping off beat, and triggering fights – jitterbugging was still a less intense, whitened version of the black-produced Lindy Hop. *Jitterbug* (originally meaning those who loved to swing dance) was coined by the trombonist-arranger Harry White but made famous by Cab Calloway and Benny Goodman.

The Nude Restaurant

Sex was central to the world of Andy Warhol (1928–87): in his fascination with youth, celebrity, and consumer desires; his flamboyant Factory happenings; his coterie of male hustlers and beautiful bohemian girls; and his arty "nudie" films. *Kiss* (1963), *Blow Job* (1964), *Taylor Meade's Ass* (1964), *The Chelsea Girls* (1966), and *Blue Movie/Fuck* (1968) all have edgy erotic themes and casts of gays, transvestites, and sexual outsiders. Billy Name, the pop artist's principal technician, made this still on the set of Warhol's *Nude Restaurant* (1967). Starring Taylor Meade and Viva, the film was shot twice at the Mad Hatter Restaurant, the first version with a totally nude all-male cast and the second with a mixed cast of actors primly wearing G-strings.

54

Studio 54 at 254 West Fifty-fourth Street was the most famous nightspot in the world from 1977 to 1980. Sensing that the protest-filled 1960s were giving way to a more hedonistic time, college buddies Steve Rubell and Ian Schrager opened one of the most lavish, chic dance clubs around. Studio 54 soon became the top sex- and drug-filled disco playground for the rich and famous and for the little people who could get past the doorman. The photographer Donna Ferrato caught the fantasyland feel of the place and time — before IRS woes closed it.

Legendary Drag

It's uncertain who came up with the idea of a day-long festival devoted to drag — Lady Bunny, Brian Butternich, Michael "Kitty" Ullman, Wendy Wild, or some of the Fleshtones — but Lady Bunny got the city's only outdoor drag fête going. In 1985 the gender-bending Wigstock (opposite) opened to a rendition of *I Feel the Earth Move*. Attendance reached fifty thousand in 1995 at the Piers. Joey Arias, on the other hand, is a one-queen show (left). A Fiorucci boutique regular and notorious downtown nightlifer, Joey successfully combined music, art, and fashion into one lifestyle and genderplay in the mid-1970s. Known for his near-perfect impersonation of his idol, Billie Holiday, here he struts at the Roxy, the longest-running, and some say the best, gay dance party in New York.

Jackie 60

Jackie 60 "is a club for dominant women, poets, gay men and lesbians, free-thinking heterosexuals, transvestites and transsexuals, fetish dressers, bisexuals, and those who love them. If you have a problem with this, please don't come in," warns this performance-oriented, underground traveling party that settled at club Mother in the meatpacking district. Jackie 60 multimedia events – one fetish soirée after another – began in 1990, the brainchild of the nightlife star Chi Chi Valente, the designer-DJ Johnny Dynell (Jackie 60 was his BDSM slave name), the dancer Richard Move, the London fashion designer Kitty Boots, and later the transgendered performer

Hattie Hathaway. Moving with the times, they created a computer-tech fetish party called Click and Drag. Other themes: the Salon de Kinky Boots, Catfight!, She-Male Reformatory, Cyber Sluts, Homo Erectus (gay archeology), Mermaids on Heroin, Asian Men of Discipline, or, at the Jackie 60 Playhouse, Cokewhore. Night of a Thousand Stevies salutes the enchantress-singer Stevie Nicks.

Gal Pals

After Stonewall, gay men and lesbians
pretty much went their separate ways.
Lesbian bars, albeit a very few compared
to gay male hangouts, cropped up
downtown, but the clientele didn't let
loose like their male counterparts until the
1980s and 90s. World-class dance clubs
like the Clit Club (right), packed with
dykes of all types — butch, femme,
political, bisexual, and lipstick — are now
much more wild pick-up spots with go-go
dancers and sexy performance art.
Scoring, unlike in the gay male world, is
not always the focus. The Cyber Sluts
(opposite) were brought into being by the
impresarios of the underground club
Jackie 60. Coining a new term, they
resurrected the sexy, psychedelic,
futuristic intergalactic queen Barbarella as
a theme for some computer-age parties.

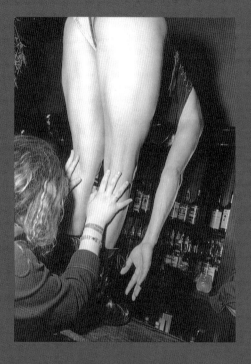

Queens of the Clubs

New York clubbers love the sexy, sharp-tongued Latina Liz Torres (above), the "Queen of House Music." One of the last great divas of dance music, this childhood church singer never had a problem drawing a crowd. Also a member of the club scene royalty is the Swiss-born, London-inspired Susanne Bartsch, the undisputed international "Queen of the Night." This legendary street-fashion originator-cum-party producer assembled a phenomenal group of drag performance artists to set the mood for her very sexy parties and raised millions for AIDS. Bartsch brought back the Harlem-style drag balls of old, helping usher in the theatrical vogueing dance trend in the early 1990s. The open air of the Chelsea Piers made Bartsch party guests get wild (opposite).

Eat It Too

Heterosexual women, according to Cake, should be free to express all aspects of their sexuality and to participate in typically male sexual entertainment. The sponsors of this women-friendly fun, Melinda Gallagher and Emily Kramer, produce monthly events "where women feel comfortable exploring sex-themed entertainment." Events like Striptease-a-thon III (right) and other sexy fashion shows, lingerie-inspired parties with explicit demonstrations, lap dancing, stripping, and porn screenings let women and their men enjoy their biggest fantasies. All men must be accompanied by women.

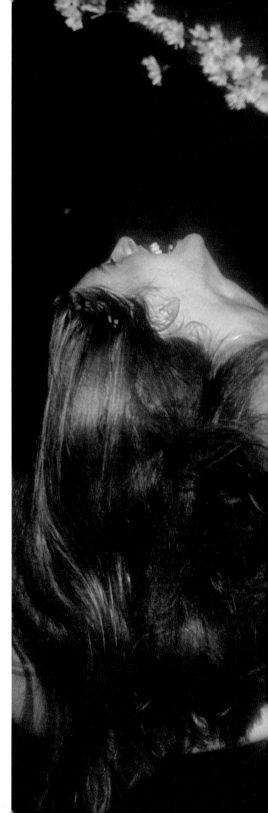

ANYTHING GOES

Beyond dreams of riches and fame, people are drawn to New York like moths to the flame of sexual freedom and the endless array of sexual possibilities. The city is big, dark, and bold enough to accommodate an intricate and diverse underground world that welcomes sexual experiences beyond mainstream straight sex. Its intense personalities are always looking for the next best thing, forming new frontiers. New Yorkers are actors, prone to theatrical displays, high drama, and fancy dress. In New York they can can get what they want when they want it, just like take-out Chinese food: strippers, more-than-massages, not-so-clean baths, live sex shows, bondage, dominance, sadomasochism, spouse swapping, cross-dressing, homosex, gender changing, orgies, interracial sex, scar and piercing rituals, masturbation clubs, sexy gourmet food, and more, all available around the corner. And then these sexual trends trickle down and out to suburbia — who can't find stylish fetish wear at the malls these days? Doris Kloster, an accomplished photographer and alternative journalist, penetrates the world of dungeons and dominations and the extraordinary universe of female sexuality. Her works, such as *Tami* (opposite), may seem strangely perverse, but Kloster's theatrical scenes, nudes, and portraits often describe the reaches of female sexual expression, from fetishism to role playing, gender bending, and playing with sex toys. Her models are powerful, real-life sex radicals. "Only in New York, kids, only in New York" (Cindy Adams). ♥

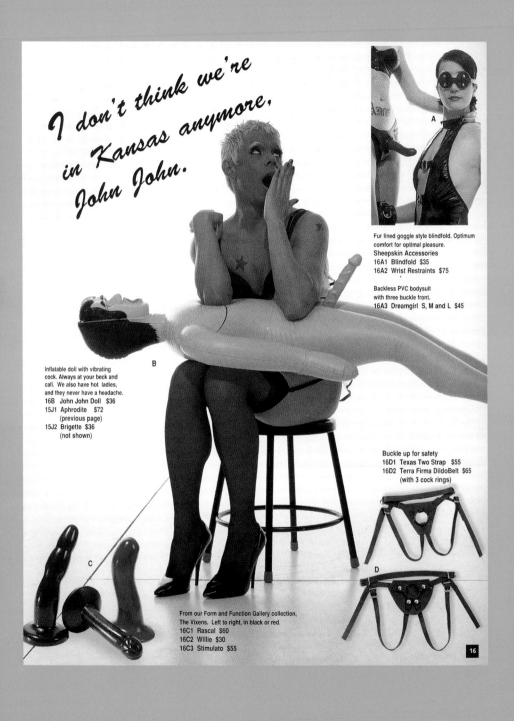

I don't think we're in Kansas anymore, John John.

A

Fur lined goggle style blindfold. Optimum comfort for optimal pleasure.
Sheepskin Accessories
16A1 Blindfold $35
16A2 Wrist Restraints $75

Backless PVC bodysuit
with three buckle front.
16A3 Dreamgirl S, M and L $45

B

Inflatable doll with vibrating cock. Always at your beck and call. We also have hot ladies, and they never have a headache.
16B John John Doll $36
15J1 Aphrodite $72
         (previous page)
15J2 Brigette $36
         (not shown)

Buckle up for safety
16D1 Texas Two Strap $55
16D2 Terra Firma DildoBelt $65
         (with 3 cock rings)

C

D

From our Form and Function Gallery collection, The Vixens. Left to right, in black or red.
16C1 Rascal $60
16C2 Willie $30
16C3 Stimulato $55

The Joys of Toys

Sex toy shops are everywhere now, but there was a time when a trip to the big city was a must for someone looking for dildos, cock rings, lubricants, harnesses, strap-ons, vibrators, and butt plugs. According to the Sex in America Survey (1994), about one in five Americans is interested in vibrators and other sex toys — typically women in their twenties. The Pleasure Chest (catalogue opposite), which opened in the West Village in 1972, brought sexual playthings out of hiding. Joined by shops such as Eve's Garden and Toys in Babeland, the Chest even offers high-tech G-spot probes. Now adult book and video stores are fighting restrictions on businesses that exhibit an "ongoing focus on sexually explicit material."

The Biggest Sex Feast in the World

Not until Frank Pernice and Larry Levinson opened Plato's Retreat in New York in 1977 did the East Coast have its own California-style swingers club. Located in the defunct gay Continental Baths in the Ansonia Hotel on West Seventy-fourth Street, the club held three hundred couples who could swap mates, have group sex, swim in a large pool, party in the Jacuzzi for twelve, act out sexual fantasies in public, or simply gawk at all of the nude bodies running around America's number one sex club. And then in 1985 Mayor Ed Koch, under the AIDS Prevention Bathhouse Law, padlocked Plato's.

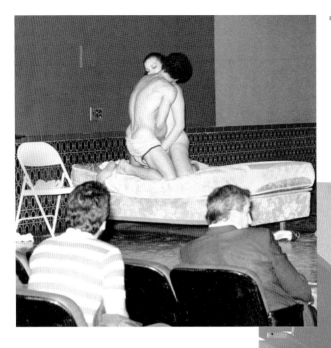

Show World

Manhattan's biggest sex venue from the
mid-1970s through the 1980s was Show
World at Times Square. Here a love team
occupies the Triple Treat Theater (above),
while on the Penthouse one found show-
girls in fantasy booths, called "live nude
reviews." In the basement were live sex
and transvestites. Employee Guy Gonzales
liked the four-tokens-for-a-dollar deal.
When the "Crossroads of the World" was
homogenized and Disneyfied, Show World
tamed its tone, keeping its video booths.

Slurpees at 711

Available twenty-four hours a day! At 711 Seventh Avenue love teams did tricks for twenty-minute turns, while men fed in quarters to keep the peep-a-round show going. These secret establishments were dramatized in Madonna's pioneering 1986 video, *Open Your Heart*.

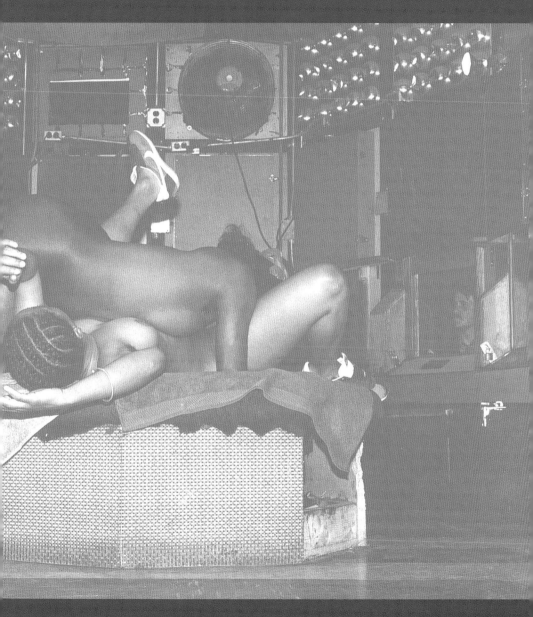

Whipping Girl

With so many high-powered execs in New York stressed out from being in charge all day long, dominatrixes are big business. For around $300 a half hour, these men can leave work and visit a leather- or latex-clad, whip-wielding tough cookie who will tell him what to do for sure. Eva Norvind, one of America's leading dominatrixes, has an accessible midtown dungeon for a little midday scolding. Another whipping girl, Emily (shown here in her Chelsea loft), looms about seven feet high in her spiked heels, but she ended up getting out of the business when she married a client. A bossy wife? Now that's a new concept.

Eulenspiegel

New York's Eulenspiegel Society is the place for those who can relate to the lad from German folklore, Til Eulenspiegel, who enjoys the effort of climbing steep hills but frowns when striding down. Founded informally in 1971 by masochists for masochists, this nonprofit organization sponsors leather, S&M, and fetish events and workshops. Now it is America's largest BDSM (bondage and discipline/dominance and submission/sadism and masochism) support group. The Eulenspiegel Society is dedicated to "supporting sexual liberation as a basic requirement of a truly free society." At its play parties, you'll have a good time or you won't have a good time — whichever way you want it.

A Suffocating Relationship

On their foray into New York's sex industry for their book *Red Light* (1996), the intrepid photographer Silvia Plachy and writer James Ridgeway found Rena Mason, a horror-movie costumer and specialist dominatrix who helps people work out their deep-seated fears and "quirks." Ridgeway recounts one client's near-death experience: After disrobing totally, he placed himself in a wooden coffin. His "mistress" then wrapped his body in plastic wrap with weak breakaway areas, just in case. At first, the plastic did not totally cover his genitals when she began pouring the wet cement, so the client cried out that his groin was too hot. Ms. Rena left an air hole in the pseudo-mummy, which she periodically covered with her foot, for him to kiss. After being left for two hours, the man was ready to be released, which the good mistress did in her own good time.

A Fine Line

Barbara Alper, an underground scene photographer, caught this violent-looking sight at a Dressing for Pleasure party sponsored by the Fetish Factor in 1992 at what is now Lucky Cheng's drag-queen restaurant in the East Village. In actuality, this is not an extreme fetish but rather a bit of light sadomasochistic activity to enhance the usual sexual activity of committed couples. For outsiders, it is hard to distinguish play from cruelty, although at fetish clubs and parties around town, participants think of it as a way to blow off steam while demonstrating trust with a loving partner.

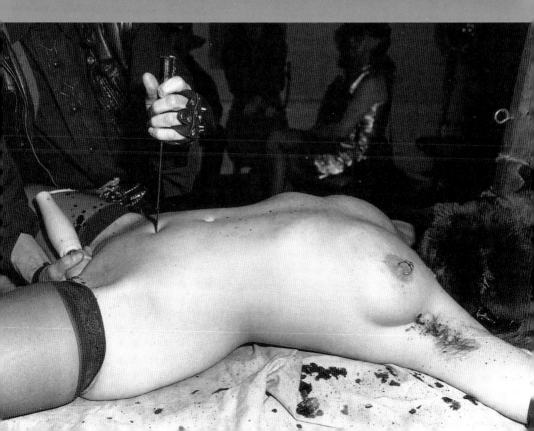

Safe Sex

A group of guys who liked to "jack off" together formalized themselves in 1980 as the New York Jacks, a progenitor of others worldwide (opposite). The Jacks started having "meatings" three days a week at various clubs, with theme parties such as a no-pants disco dance once a month. While they encourage nudity, exhibitionism, and voyeurism, they prohibit "insertion of anyone's anything into anywhere." There is no alcohol — only unscented Albolene and paper towels. For more safe sex, including spanking, there is the Hellfire, New York's original BDSM fetish fantasy club (above). Hellfire holds slave auctions and special parties, such as the hot one given in 2001 by the underground sex-world aficionado Michele Capozzi. For all persuasions, the club offers dungeons, jail cells, stocks, crosses, and other bondage equipment. "Remember to always play safely," admonishes the management. "We expect you to be on your best behavior," which means no alcohol or drugs, no oral sex, no anal or vaginal sex, no tongues, and insertables must be covered in latex.

Packing It

After Shelly Mars made an art out of acting manly in
her role as Ramona/Martin in Monika Treut's 1988 film
The Virgin Machine, New York became a drag king capital
(a term coined by the makeup artist Johnny Science).
With her drag king workshops, the New York "gender-
tainer" Diane Torr really turned female-to-male cross-
dressing into a phenomenon of "self-awareness," mainly
for young lesbian women. Other notorious kings are Labio
(Fabio's younger brother), Dréd and Lizeracé, and Murray
Hill, known for his Ralph Camdenesque macho schtick and
for his campaign for mayor against Rudolph Giuliani in
1997. Mo B. Dick (right) launched Club Casanova, the first
weekly drag-king night in the United States for women
who want to "honor" men, even though they sometimes
play seedy characters, by strapping in their breasts and
wearing jock straps packed with socks or dildos.

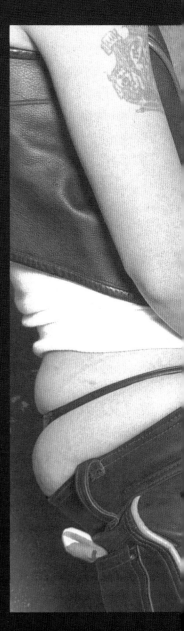

Boys Who Want to Be Girls

New York is probably the easiest place in America to transform oneself. In 1952, when the nation was full of anxiety about homosexuality in the military, the news hit the country: "Ex GI Becomes Blond Beauty : Operations Transform Bronx Youth" *(New York Post).* From boyhood George Jorgensen (1926–89) had thought he was really a girl. He went to Denmark, where Dr. Hamburger performed an orchiectomy and a penectomy — and George came back as the charismatic Christine. (A vagina was created a few years later.) Christine wanted to live quietly on Long Island, but she couldn't resist the lucrative nightclub business (below). What was missing was an academy for boys who want to be girls, a void filled in 1993 by Veronica Vera, a writer and lecturer on human sexuality, a model for Robert Mapplethorpe, and an X-rated film star. To help men "experience the sensual pleasure of their femme-selves," her Chelsea school offers courses on makeup, clothing, carriage, and speech in private sessions or in weekend on-the-town experiences (opposite). Eighty percent of Vera's students are straight.

Miss Vera's Finishing School for *Boys* Who Want to Be *Girls*

Tips, Tales, & Teachings from the Dean of the World's First Cross-Dressing Academy

❖ ❖ ❖ ❖ **Veronica Vera** ❖ ❖ ❖ ❖

Magic Act

Male-to-female trannie stars Amanda Lepore and Sophia
LaMar perform a special act for people who need more
than just the sight of two very exotic girls: they pull
scarves and toy rabbits out of the most amazing places.
When they lost their dancing jobs at Twilo in 2001
because the club wanted to switch to "biological girls,"
the duo sued, citing emotional distress, humiliation, and
damage to their careers and reputations.

S O U R C E S

PART I: LIVE AND LET LIVE

Real Men and Women Who Were Too
Page 15. "Amerindian women who had sex ... political ties with natives": Evan Haefeli, Princeton University, Princeton, N.J. "Lenape, or 'Real Men'. . . .": Eric Homberger, *The Historical Atlas of New York City: A Visual Celebration of Nearly 400 Years of New York City's History* (New York: Henry Holt, 1994), p. 16. "Director-General Willem Kieft strictly enforced ... general lack of regard for chastity": Edwin G. Burrows and Mike Wallace, *Gotham: A History of New York City to 1898* (New York: Oxford University Press, 1999), pp. 31–32, 34. **Page 16.** "The Dutch Calvinists had strict sexual customs ... yet a wife was never her husband's equal": Edwin G. Burrows and Mike Wallace, *Gotham*, pp. 51–52. "... as in Amsterdam, 'bawds' and 'doxies' ... Two pound butter's whore!'": Edwin G. Burrows and Mike Wallace, *Gotham*, pg. 34. **Page 18.** "Two weeks before ... fifty or a hundred names": *Valentine's Manual of Old New York*, vol. 10 (New York: Valentine's Manual, Inc., 1926), p. 49. "... adorned with trinkets and ribbons ... happy New Year": Richard Gooch, "America and the Americans in 1833–34," <http://xroads.virginia.edu/~HYPER/DETOC/FEM/gooch.htm> (April 2002). "... the men rushed madly ... total up all their cards": *Valentine's Manual of Old New York*, vol. 10, p. 49. "Every house became ... kisses all given gratis": Richard Gooch, "America and the Americans in 1833–34." "New York Harbor and the surrounding ... dub the area Pearl Street": Eric Homberger, *The Historical Atlas of New York City*, p. 16. **Page 21.** "... family became the central economic unit ... for exploring sexual desires": John D'Emilio and Estelle B. Freedman, *Intimate Matters: A History of Sexuality in America* (Chicago: University of Chicago Press, 1988, 1997), pp. 15–21. "A suitor who traveled a long distance ... were expected to marry": John D'Emilio and Estelle B. Freedman, *Intimate Matters*, pp. 16–22. "Bundling prevailed for at least ... required a five-year waiting period": Bradley Smith, *The American Way of Sex: An Informal Illustrated History* (New York: Two Continents, 1978), pp. 53, 57.

Class Acts
Page 23. "The British leisure class ... crass language": Edwin G. Burrows and Mike Wallace, *Gotham*, pp. 172–75. "Women's fashions ... untamed place": Lloyd Morris, *Incredible New York: High Life and Low Life from 1850 to 1950* (Syracuse: Syracuse University Press, 1951). "... Third Avenue world of the respectable poor": Lloyd Morris, *Incredible New York*. "In this 'go ahead' age ...": Bradley Smith, *The American Way of Sex*. **Page 24.** Edwin G. Burrows and Mike Wallace,

Gotham, pp. 50–54. **Page 25.** "Dr. Alexander Hamilton remarked ... aboard anchored ships": Edwin G. Burrows and Mike Wallace, *Gotham*, p. 185. **Page 27.** "The governor of New York ... fondle his wife's ears": Henry Moscow, *The Book of New York Firsts* (Syracuse: Syracuse University Press, 1995). "The portrait ... took charge of the city": Patricia Bonomi, *The Lord Cornbury Scandal: The Politics of Reputation in British America* (Chapel Hill: University of North Carolina Press, for the Omohundro Institute of Early American History and Culture, Williamsburg, Va., 1998). "He was a deadbeat ... earl of Clarendon": Edwin G. Burrows and Mike Wallace, *Gotham*, p. 115. **Page 29.** "Fanny Hill acquired a bad name ... like this one from 1776": Marianna Beck, "The Roots of Western Pornography," part 3. England Bites Back with Fanny Hill," *Libido Magazine* <www.libidomag.com/nakedbrunch/europorn07.html>. "Rumor had it that ... and 'abyss of joy'": Mariana Beck, "The Roots of Western Pornography." "In 1821 ... for wider enjoyment": John Cleland, "Memoirs of a Woman of Pleasure ..." <www.thefileroom.org/FileRoom/documents/Cases/171cleland.htm> (April 2002). **Page 30.** "A lonely guy might have ... spell out CUNT": Milton Simpson, *Folk Erotica: Celebrating Centuries of Erotic Americana* (New York: HarperCollins, 1994), pp. 22–23. "Lieutenant Isaac Bangs ... 'brutal creatures'": Timothy J. Gilfoyle, *City of Eros: New York City, Prostitution, and the Commercialization of Sex, 1790–1920* (New York: W. W. Norton, 1992), pp. 23–25. "During the British occupation of the City ... in the fire of 1776": Edwin G. Burrows and Mike Wallace, *Gotham*, p. 229. "City-wide whorehouse riots ... strangers on big-city streets": Christine Stansell, *City of Women: Sex and Class in New York 1789–1860* (New York: Knopf, 1986), p. 24–26, quoted in John D'Emilio and Estelle B. Freedman, *Intimate Matters*, p. 39. **Page 32.** "During the Revolutionary War ... redcoats paved the way": Bradley Smith, *The American Way of Sex*, pp. 65–67. "British men were smitten ... amorous affairs with her friends": Linda Grant De Pauw, *Four Traditions: Women of New York During the American Revolution* (Albany: New York State American Revolution Bicentennial Commission, 1974), pp. 25–27. 30. "General Howe, she noted ... who was his mistress": Bradley Smith, *The American Way of Sex*, pp. 65–67. "The Baroness ... houses and bad company": Linda Grant De Pauw, *Four Traditions*, pp. 25–30. **Page 34.** "... smart ensemble worn by refined New Yorkers": Edwin G. Burrows and Mike Wallace, *Gotham*, pp. 172–75. "This ivory satin example ... Hamilton's wife, Elizabeth": Barbara Parent, guest curator, "The Museum of the City of New York Presents a Virtual Exhibition of Women's Eighteenth Century Shoes," <www.mcny.org>. "To distinguish

themselves ... serving girls and prostitutes": Edwin G. Burrows and Mike Wallace, *Gotham*, pp. 172–75. **Page 35.** "An illegitimate child ... was rich and powerful": "National Archives Biography of Alexander Hamilton," <www.jmu.edu/madison/hamilton.htm> (April 2002). "After he became ... leave her abusive husband": "Back to Contemporary Controversies, Political Scandal in Historical Perspective," Gilder Lehrman History Online, <www.gliah.uh.edu/historyonline/scandal.cfm> (April 2002). "... instead to blackmail Hamilton ... the Treasury Department": Bradley Smith, *The American Way of Sex*, p. 63. "Although he paid ... peers such as George Washington": "Back to Contemporary Controversies, Political Scandal in Historical Perspective," Gilder Lehrman History Online, <www.gliah.uh.edu/historyonline/scandal.cfm> (April 2002). **Page 36.** "Usually sold under the counter ... 'Of Monstrous Births' was included": John D'Emilio and Estelle B. Freedman, *Intimate Matters*, pp. 19–20. "Fruits of the labor" and "Of Monstrous Births": *Aristotle's Compleat Masterpiece* (New York, 1788), p. 58. **Page 37.** "With its details ... only servant in the house": Bradley Smith, *The American Way of Sex*, pp. 66–69. **Page 38.** "About 7,500 free blacks ... found a way to freedom": Edwin G. Burrows and Mike Wallace, *Gotham*, pp. 31, 33, 40, 44, 49, 53–56, 308, 347–49. "To justify continued economic and social subordination of blacks ... opposed interracial blending": John D'Emilio and Estelle B. Freedman, *Intimate Matters*, pp. 13, 14, 35, 37. "... the word *miscegenation* ...": Richard Newman, "History/Miscegenation," <www.africana.com/Utilities/Content.html?&../cgi-bin/banner.pl?banner=Education&../Articles/tt_425.htm> (April 2002). "White men who desired ... were lustful and easy": John D'Emilio and Estelle. B. Freedman, *Intimate Matters*, pp. 13, 14, 35, 37. **Pages 40–41.** "America's first slum ...": Ted Widmer, "Slumming in Squeeze Gut Alley. The Story of the Dirtiest Ward," *New York Observer*, August 20, 2001. "...'shoulder hitters', tramps ... transients and prostitutes": Timothy J. Gilfoyle, *City of Eros*, pp. 36–46. "The reporter George Foster ... the family's one room": George Foster, "The Points at Midnight," *New York by Gaslight*, no. VII, 1850. "Newspapers fueled white fears ... other local entrepreneurs": Timothy J. Gilfoyle, *City of Eros*, pp. 36–46. **Page 43.** "Working-class men bored ... to East Fourth Street": David M. Stewart, *Consuming Working Class Masculinity* (Taiwan: National Central University) http://216.239.51.100/search?q=cache:K8Jk7d-LFG4C:info.pue.udlap.mx/congress/5/papers_pdf/dms.pdf+Stewart,+David+M.,+Consuming+Working+Class+Masculinity,+National+Central+University,+Taiwan&hl=en&ie=UTF-8> (April 2002).

"'B'hoys' was a general handle ... dance halls, and brothels": Edwin G. Burrows and Mike Wallace, *Gotham*, pp. 633–34, 753, 758–59. "They swaggered about ... Broadway cultural elite": Lloyd Morris, *Incredible New York*, pp. 34–38. "Dressed like 'fancy-dans' ... requisite stogie": Edwin G. Burrows and Mike Wallace, *Gotham*, pp. 633–34, 753, 758–59. "Mose, the hero ... by the upper class": David M. Stewart, "Consuming Working Class Masculinity." "Bowery G'hals ... on their heads": Lloyd Morris, *Incredible New York*, pp. 34–38. "Although neighborhood gangs ... against prostitutes and madams.": Timothy J. Gilfoyle, *City of Eros*, pp. 87, 90, 110, 115. **Page 44.** "Cramped tenements ... populate urban areas": Lloyd Morris, *Incredible New York*, pp. 274–77. "New York had at least 43,000 ... more than 1.5 million persons": Eric Homberger, *The Historical Atlas of New York City*, p. 110–11. "A family might live ... exacerbated the problems": Lloyd Morris, *Incredible New York*, pp. 274–77.

Separate Spheres

Page 46. "After the revolution ... close to hunky workmen": Edwin G. Burrows and Mike Wallace, *Gotham*, pp. 283–84, 796. "The 'sporting male' (confirmed bachelor) ... riots in the 1830s": Timothy J. Gilfoyle, *City of Eros*, pp. 81–84, 115–16, 119, 20, 145–46, 181, 195, 236–39, 313–14, 327. **Page 48.** "Most middle-class women ... vacationing together": Edwin G. Burrows and Mike Wallace, *Gotham*, pp. 283–84, 796. "One woman who ventured out ... several moral guidance books": "Sedgwick, Catherine Maria" <http://search.biography.com/print_record.pl?id=19323> (April 2002). "Fifteen years later ... public was outraged.": Lloyd Morris, *Incredible New York*, pp. 86–88. **Page 50.** "Known for his tragic roles ... after each performance": Lloyd Morris, *Incredible New York*, pp. 62–63. Pages 52–53. "The nineteenth century ... tough decision for any wife": John D'Emilio and Estelle. B. Freedman, *Intimate Matters*, pp. 55–57. **Page 55.** "Douglass had come to New York ... Mount Holyoke Seminary": Beverly McClure, <http://216.239.51.100/search?q=cache:h-h0dUKpAAAC.faculty.stcc.cc.tn.us/bmcclure/lessons2/douglass.htm+Beverly+McClure+Frederick+Douglass&hl=en&ie=UTF-8> (April 2002). "For Douglass ... and given no offense": The Life of Frederick Douglass," National Park Service, <www.nps.gov/frdo/fdlife.htm> (April 2002). **Page 56.** "As the twentieth century dawned ... and boiled shirts": Lloyd Morris, *Incredible New York*, pp. 211–12. "The Gibson Girl ... set the style of the era": "History of the Gibson Girl," <www.geocities.com/gibsongirls2001/paarticle1.html> (April 2002). "Trying to make one's waist ... virtue and refinement": Christina Larson, "Of Corset Matters," a review of Valerie Steele's *The Corset: A Cultural History*, The Washington Monthly Online, 2001 <www.washingtonmonthly.com/features/2001/0201.larson.html> (April 2002). "... even if doctors

... impaired fertility": Valerie Steele, *The Corset: A Cultural History* (New Haven: Yale University Press, 2001). "Women themselves ... within their own sex": Christina Larson, "Of Corset Matters," 2001.

Scandalous Extremes

Page 58. "... in 1836 was quickly ... sexuality, gender, and class": Timothy Gilfoyle, *City of Eros*, pp. 44, 73, 92–98, 100–101, 141, 145, 151. "In 1841, Mary Rogers ... committed suicides": "Woodhull and Claflin's Weekly Upward and Onward," September 16, 1871, from *She Is More to Be Pitied than Censured: Women, Sexuality and Murder in 19th Century America* (exhibition from the collections of the John Hay Library, April 1–May 15, 1996), <www.brown.edu/Facilities/University_Library/exhibits/RLCexhibit/bowlsby/bowlsbyms.html> (April 2002). "On the premise that lust ... literature out of circulation": John D'Emilio and Estelle B. Freedman, *Intimate Matters*, 60–61, 66, 140, 146–47, 156–57, 159–64, 174, 203, 206, 222–23, 232, 242, 277, 284. "In 1873 Comstock ... odius books": Bradley Smith, *The American Way of Sex*, pp. 95, 98, 139, 157. "For a time ... drove them away": John D'Emilio and Estelle B. Freedman, *Intimate Matters*, 60–61, 66, 140, 146–47, 156–57, 159–64, 174, 203, 206, 222–23, 232, 242, 277, 284. **Page 60.** "In April 1836 ... set on fire": Patricia Cline Cohen, *The Murder of Helen Jewett* (New York: Vintage Books, 1998). "Richard Robinson ... 41 Thomas Street": Timothy J. Gilfoyle, *City of Eros*, pp. 44, 73, 92–98, 100–101, 141, 145, 151. "The public was divided ... was quickly acquitted": Timothy J. Gilfoyle, *City of Eros*, pp. 44, 73, 92–98, 100–101, 141, 145, 151. **Page 62.** "The Übermensch 'sporting press' ... be interested in his clothes": Timothy Gilfoyle, *City of Eros*, pp. 135–37. "Abominable sinners": *The Whip*, February 5, 1842, quoted in Timothy J. Gilfoyle, *City of Eros*, p. 136. "... beasts who follow that unhallowed practice": *The Whip*, February 12, 1842, quoted in Timothy J. Gilfoyle, *City of Eros*, pp. 136. **Page 65.** "Utopian communities ... sexual impulses": John D'Emilio and Estelle B. Freedman, *Intimate Matters*, 112–17. "Brooklyn founded by ... hostility within and outside": Randall Hillebrand, "The Shakers / Oneida Community," <www.seii.com/ccn/cults/othr09b.txt> (May 2002). **Page 66.** "She solved the problems ... (Ann Lohman)": Timothy J. Gilfoyle, *City of Eros*, pp. 135, 143–44. "... built her successful ... causing her suicide": Lloyd Morris, *Incredible New York*, pp. 45–56. **Page 68.** "Emphasizing love and desire ... encouraging women's equality": John D'Emilio and Estelle B. Freedman, *Intimate Matters*, pp. 109, 111–116, 120, 138, 156–57, 161–67, 278. "... but her free-love platform ... caught at William Sanger's trial": John D'Emilio and Estelle B. Freedman, *Intimate Matters*, 60–61, 66, 140, 146–57, 159–64, 174, 203, 206, 222–23, 232, 242, 277, 284. **Page 71.** "... the era's most influential ... show up at her event": Bradley Smith, *The American Way of

Sex*, pp. 94–95. "Next she tried ... called him a hypocrite": John D'Emilio and Estelle B. Freedman, *Intimate Matters*, p. 163. "Elizabeth Tilton's love for Beecher ... sent up the river": Bradley Smith, *The American Way of Sex*, pp. 94–95. **Page 73.** "Evelyn Nesbit was in great demand ... horsewhipping a young boy": Bradley Smith, *The American Way of Sex*, pp. 138–40. **Page 74.** "On August 26, 1986 ... up for parole in December 2002)": Mark Gado, "A Killing in Central Park: The Preppy Murder Case," <www.crimelibrary.com/classics5/preppy/index.htm> (May 24, 2002). **Page 75.** "... now a cable TV show host ... Albion Correctional Facility in New York": "Amy Fisher Released from Prison Monday, May 10, 1999," <www.geocities.com/Hollywood/Interview/4557/newstribune_05_10_99.html> (May 24, 2002).

Sex Ed and Med

Page 77. "Before the twentieth century ... was the path of righteousness": Edwin G. Burrows and Mike Wallace, *Gotham*, pp. 589–90. " In the early 1830s ... ability to fight disease": "Porn Flakes: Kellogg, Graham and the Crusade for Moral Fiber" <http://www.ibiblio.org/stayfree/10/graham.htm> (May 25, 2002). "Enter Margaret Sanger ... motherhood and feminine virtue": *The Papers of Margaret Sanger*, ed. Esther Katz et al. (Columbia, S.C.: Model Editions Partnership, 1999), <http://adh.sc.edu> (May 24, 2002). **Page 78.** "The 1873 Comstock Law ... other 'hygiene' products": Andrea Tone, *Devices and Desires: A History of Contraceptives in America* (New York: Hill and Wang, 2001), pp. 13–14. "Condoms finally received the stamp ... American Condom Empire": Andrea Tone, *Devices and Desires*, pp. 184–87. **Page 81.** "American doughboys were the only ... unable to 'just say no'": Jon Knowles, "Notes on the History of the Condom" <www.plannedparenthood.org/condoms/history.html> (May 28, 2002). "In the early 1960s, Mary ... and its freedom from exploitation": Debra W. Haffner, "From the President: SIECUS at 35," vol. 27, no. 4, <www.siecus.org/pubs/srpt/srpt0020.html> (May 29, 2002). **Page 82.** "For women who suffered ... prohibition of masturbation": Linda Meyers, "Rachel Maines' Book in History of Vibrator Garners Two Awards," <www.news.cornell.edu/Chronicle/00/3.30.00/Maines_book.html> (June 9, 2002). "... did their duty ... scene in the 1880s": Rachel Maines, "Socially Camouflaged Technologies: The Case of the Electromechanical Vibrator," *IEEE Technology and Society Magazine*, vol. 8, no. 2, June 1989, as cited in "History of the Vibrator," Urban Legends, <www.urbanlegends.com/sex/history_of_the_vibrator.html> (June 9, 2002). "Early vibrators were advertised ... for women's health": Linda Meyers, "Rachel Maines' Book in History of Vibrator Garners Two Awards." "These devices were fifth ... kettle and toaster": Natalie Angier, "In the History of Gynecology, a Surprising

Chapter," *New York Times*, February 23, 1999.
Page 83. "Katherine Bement Davis . . . Anita
Newcomb McGee (1888–91)": "First Female
Sexologist," <www.world-sex-records.com/sex-
004.htm> (May 29, 2002). **Page 85.** ". . . learned
to make a beautiful . . . through the Charles Atlas
program": "Modern Classics, Art Photographs
of Tony Sansone," 1932, <www.geocities.com/
WestHollywood/Heights/8052/sansone1.<html>
(May 29, 2002). "This living Greek statue . . .
gymnasiums around New York": "Edwin F.
Townsend/Sansone," <www.bigkugels.com/
content/Towsend.html> (May 29, 2002).
"The Italian American . . . booklets in the 1930s":
"Modern Classics, Art Photographs of Tony
Sansone," 1932. **Page 87.** "Sex workers and
dancers . . . 'we can tighten them up.'": James
Ridgeway and Sylvia Plachy, *Red Light: Inside the
Sex Industry* (New York: Powerhouse Books, 1996),
pp. 183–87.

PART II: SCENE AND BE SEEN

A Wide-Open Town

Page 90. "After debuting in vaudeville . . . Tassel
Twirler in 1929": *The Real Gypsy Rose Lee*, <www.
geocities.com/vickie_alonzo/gypsy.html>
(May 31, 2002). "She was a slow stripper . . . down
to a G-string": Bradley Smith, *The American Way
of Sex*, pp. 179–80. **Page 93.** "Lola Montez
brought her passionate . . . her dirty dancing":
Lloyd Morris, *Incredible New York*, pp. 61–62.
"In her tarantula . . . beat off rowdy spectators":
Jeff Woloson, "Lola Montez," <http://home2.
planetinternet.be/verjans/Society_Divas/
lola_montez_a.htm> (June 4, 2002). "After
success in San Francisco . . . packing to the Bowery
Theater": Lloyd Morris, *Incredible New York*,
pp. 61–62. "Lola died . . . a decade later":
"Lola Montez (E Clampus Vitus—Credo Quia
Absurdum)," <www.sonnet.com/eqdir/clamper/
Lola.html> (June 4, 2002). **Page 94.** "To Mark
Twain, they were . . . paintings and classical
sculpture": Timothy Gilfoyle, *City of Eros*, pp.
127–29. "Scenes usually depicted . . . the Three
Graces": "The History of Tableaux Vivants,"
<http://homepages.msn.com/LibraryLawn/
auguster/rohrbach/Russo/tableaux.html>
(June 5, 2002). "Some theaters had revolving . . .
great self-discipline": Timothy Gilfoyle, *City of
Eros*, pp. 127–29. **Page 96.** "Less reputable
museums . . . one might find": Timothy Gilfoyle,
City of Eros, pp. 127, 230–31. ". . . 'figures of men
and women . . . groups, attitudes and positions'":
District Attorney Indictment Papers, Court of
General Sessions, New York City Municipal
Archives and Records Center, *People v. Beach*, 22
November, 1850, cited in Timothy Gilfoyle, *City of
Eros*, p. 230. ". . . models of reproductive organs . . .
her elegance and loveliness": District Attorney
Indictment Papers, Court of General Sessions,
cited in Timothy Gilfoyle, *City of Eros*, p. 127.

Page 98. "Lillian Russell . . . gilded and bejeweled
bicycles": Lloyd Morris, *Incredible New York*, pp. 68,
189, 214, 226, 238, 261, 264–65, 269. "Russell
found herself . . . wear tights while performing":
Bradley Smith, *The American Way of Sex*, p. 137–38.
Page 100. ". . . masquerade balls sponsored by . . .
public propriety": Timothy Gilfoyle, *City of Eros*,
pp. 130, 232–36, 250. ". . . concert saloons . . .
vaudeville, and Italian opera": Timothy Gilfoyle,
City of Eros, pp. 129, 141, 189–90, 224–32, 253,
367. "The biggest attraction was . . . highly visible
in church": Lloyd Morris, *Incredible New York*, pp.
48–52, 72. **Page 103.** "In the early to mid-1800s . .
. offered the ladies a little titillation": John A.
Kenrick, "History of the Musical: Variety, Honky-
tonks, and Vaudeville," <musicals101.com>
(June 2002). **Page 104.** "To get away from the
bourgeois world . . . the worst dive in town":
George Chauncey, *Gay New York: Gender, Urban
Culture and the Making of the Gay Male World,
1890–1940* (New York: Basic Books, 1994), pp.
36–37. ". . . the Reverend Charles Parkhurst went
slumming . . . Ta-ra-ra Boom-de-ay": Edwin G.
Burrows and Mike Wallace, *Gotham*, pp. 1167–69.
Page 106. "Ever since the Gilded Age . . .
love affair with food": "Fine Dining," <http://
www.nyfoodmuseum.org/> (June 8, 2002).
"Flamboyantly effeminate men . . . most
degenerate spot in the city": George Chauncey,
Gay New York, pp. 32–34, 36–45, 47, 68, 79–86,
138, 149, 162. "New York nightlife . . . century's
first decade": Lloyd Morris, *Incredible New York*,
pp. 317–18. "In these descendants of concert
saloons . . . a large dance space": Timothy Gilfoyle,
City of Eros, pp. 247–50, 258–88, 402. ". . . teams
performed and couples . . . and tango": Lloyd
Morris, *Incredible New York*, pp. 317–18. "A lot of
sexually charged . . . prostitutes was played down":
Timothy Gilfoyle, *City of Eros*, pp. 247–50,
258–88, 402. "Murray's Roman Gardens . . . all its
decadent grandeur": Rem Koolhaas, *Delirious New
York: A Retroactive Manifesto for Manhattan* (New
York: Oxford University Press, 1978), pp. 82–85.
Page 108. "The Haymarket on Sixth Avenue . . .
attracted a varied crowd": Timothy Gilfoyle, *City
of Eros*, pp. 205, 220, 227–28, 253, 258, 314.
"'Diamond Jim' Brady . . . sans his baubles": Lloyd
Morris, *Incredible New York*, pp. 220–21. "The
saloon was one of a number . . . named with
European flair": Timothy Gilfoyle, *City of Eros*,
pp. 205, 220, 227–28, 253, 258, 314. "Good style
reigned outside . . . sex or naughty circuses":
Edwin G. Burrows and Mike Wallace, *Gotham*,
p. 148. **Page 111.** "With the premiere of movie
theaters . . . palaces of pleasure": John D'Emilio
and Estelle B. Freedman, *Intimate Matters*,
pp. 195–97. ". . . piano music helped set the scene
. . . notorious back rows": Bradley Smith, *The
American Way of Sex*, p. 208. "Feature films . . .
encouraged independence": John D'Emilio and
Estelle B. Freedman, *Intimate Matters*, pp. 195–97.
"Before the Hays Code (1934) . . . attracted big
crowds": Tim Dirks, "Sexual or Erotic Films,"

<www.filmsite.org/sexualfilms.html> (June 9,
2002). "Young men who could afford . . . exchange
for sexual favors": John D'Emilio and Estelle B.
Freedman, *Intimate Matters*, pp. 195–97. **Page
112.** "The legendary showman, Florenz Ziegfeld
. . . Ziggy's girls": John Kenrick, "History of the
Musical Stage, 1910–1920. Part II: Ziegfeld,"
<www.musicals101.com/1910bway2.htm>
(June 10, 2002). ". . . among them Barbara Stan-
wick . . . and Fanny Brice": "Girls of the Ziegfeld
Follies" <www.streetswing.com/histmai2/
d2zgrls1.htm> (June 10, 2002). "Fashions by Lady
Duff-Gordon . . . feminine forms": John Kenrick,
"History of the Musical Stage, 1910–1920. Part II:
Ziegfeld." "The pinup artist Alberto Vargas . . . for
the next twelve years": Louis K. Meisel and Charles
G. Martignette, *The Great American Pin-up* (New
York: Taschen, 1996), excerpted in "The Alberto
Vargas Gallery: The Pinup Files," <www.
thepinupfiles.com/vargas1.html> (June 2002).
"All in all, it was a respectable . . . could bring his
wife": John Kenrick, "History of the Musical
Stage, 1910–1920. Part II: Ziegfeld." **Page 115.**
"During World War II . . . black or white men":
Bradley Smith, *The American Way of Sex*,
pp. 223–25. "Gays especially . . . exploded in the
1960s": John D'Emilio and Estelle B. Freedman,
Intimate Matters, pp. 242, 260–61, 282, 288–90.
Page 116. "When burlesque . . . playing Times
Square theaters": "An Excerpt from Grindhouse
Burlesque," <www.noircity.com/burlesque.html>
(June 11, 2002). ". . . (from the Italian *burla*,
meaning jest)": "Music Hall, Vaudeville, and
Burlesque (1843)," <www.yk.psu.edu/~jmj3/
sna_aum3.htm> (June 11, 2002). ". . . known for
her flying G-string act . . . queens of the striptease": "Lili St. Cyr, the Queen of Burlesque,
1918–1999," <www.vivavavoom.com/girls/
lili/main.html> (June 11, 2002). "The 'bur-le-q'
survived . . . ban in 1937": "An Excerpt from
Grindhouse Burlesque." "Scores, the gentlemen's
club . . . relieve pressures of all sorts": "Scores," in
*Sexy New York City 2001: The Annual Guide to NYC
Erotica* (Brooklyn: On Your Own Publications,
2001), introduction, pp. 135, 151–52. ". . . (the
attendants are well tipped)": Christopher Byron,
"From Web Design to Topless Bars: The Fascina-
ting Tale of Internet Advisory Corp," <www.
msnbc.com/news/723667.asp> (June 11, 2002).

Demimondaines

Page 119. "It might be inconceivable . . . virtue
of decent women": Timothy Gilfoyle, *City of Eros*.
"At midcentury, Dr. William Sanger . . . of the
garment industry": Edwin G. Burrows and Mike
Wallace, *Gotham*, pp. 483–85, 803–7). "Although
prostitution wasn't all . . . and socially independent": Timothy Gilfoyle, *City of Eros*, p. 314. "The
photographer . . . canned by the local cops": Merry
Alpern, *Dirty Windows* (Zurich: Scalo Books, 1995).
Page 121. Timothy Gilfoyle, *City of Eros*, pp. 29–
54, 197–223. **Page 122.** "Ostensibly reproachful
exposés . . . most tempting brothels": Timothy

Gilfoyle, *City of Eros*, pp. 34, 131–32. "Rosina Townsend became ... Rosie doing a year for Graft": Timothy Gilfoyle, *City of Eros*, pp. 73, 258, 294. **Page 125.** "Cigar stores in particular ... more grueling industrial labor": Timothy Gilfoyle, *City of Eros*, pp. 285–88. "Julia Brown and Kate Ridgely ... elite of Bleeker Street": Timothy Gilfoyle, *City of Eros*, p. 71. "Eliza Bowen Jumel ... New York high society": Edwin G. Burrows and Mike Wallace, *Gotham*, p. 485. **Page 127.** "... the prostitute and madam became ... who victimized men": Timothy Gilfoyle, *City of Eros*, pp. 143–60. "For many women who had a hard time ... boardinghouses filled a need": Timothy Gilfoyle, *City of Eros*, pp. 161–68, 198–202, 204–5, 285. **Page 128.** "A slumming craze ... fan-tan gambling parlors": Mary Ting Yi Lui, "The Real Yellow Peril: Mapping Racial and Gender Boundaries in New York City's Chinatown, 1870–1910," *HCM, A Journal of Asian American Cultural Criticism*, vol. 5, no. 1, Spring 1998. "Chinamen, who were always ... married Irish 'apple women'": Edwin G. Burrows and Mike Wallace, *Gotham*, pp. 1126–31. "Because the Chinese culture ... trap white women": Mary Ting Yi Lui, *The Real Yellow Peril*, and Edwin G. Burrows and Mike Wallace, *Gotham*, pp. 1126–31. "Even second-hand smoke ...'The Real Yellow Peril'": Mary Ting Yi Lui, *The Real Yellow Peril*. **Page 131.** "Voted Holland's best secretary ... in her Amsterdam home": "Xaviera Hollander: The Woman Behind the Myth," <www. xavierahollander.com/start.html> (June 11, 2002). **Page 132.** "... cared enough to offer them ... two-hour session": "In the Matter of Sydney Biddle Barrows, a Witness Before the President's Commission on Organized Crime," <www. thesmokinggun.com/archive/barrows1.shtml> (June 12, 2002). **Page 133.** "Inspired as a young girl ... doubles and multiples": Sandy Naiman, "Dear Diary: Ottawa Woman's Call Girl Confessions," *Toronto Sun*, November 12, 2001. **Page 134.** "Times Square in the 1920s ... Seventh and Eighth Avenues": "TIMES2: Recreation at the Crossroads of the World, Commercial Entertainment," <http://216.239. 35.100/search?q=cache:CdsTFhJyhBIC:home. luna.nl/~xino/times2/ts04.htm+Male+Hustlers+ New+York+City&hl=en> (June 19, 2002). "... the 'Deuce' ... unusual characters took over": "Times Square: A Gay History," <http://huzbears. websitenow.com/gayhistory/ts.html> (June 19, 2002). "But not all hustlers ... usually the biggest risk": Donald Suggs, "Bargaining Power: Safer Sex and Survival on the Streets of New York," <:www.poz.com/archive/september1998/inside/ bargaining.html+Male+Hustlers+New+York+City &hl=enz> (June 19, 2002).

Escapes

Page 137. "Manhattan went from a city ... escape became urgent": Rem Koolhaas, *Delirious New York*, p. 17. "In the 1830s, and even ... transportation got better": Eric Homberger, *The Historical Atlas of*

New York City, pp. 128–29. "New Yorkers began heading to ... romance and lust": Rem Koolhaas, *Delirious New York*, p. 17. "Cars were machines of escape ... transition to adulthood": Glenn Dawes, "Time to Ride: Youth and the Culture of Joyriding in Rural Queensland" (Townsville: James Cook University) <www.aic.gov.au/conferences/ regional/dawes.pdf+Automobile+escape+for+ youth&rhl=en> (June 5, 2002). **Page 139.** "Central Park, New York's in-town rural ... city's grand dowagers": Lloyd Morris, *Incredible New York*, pp. 91–98. **Page 141.** "In 1869 the railroad finally made Coney Island accessible": Eric Homberger, *The Historical Atlas of New York City*, pp. 128–29. "... called by the architect ... entrance of New York Harbor": Rem Koolhaas, *Delirious New York*, pp. 23–29. "... with great beaches ... pleasures in sleazy areas": Lloyd Morris, *Incredible New York*, pp. 91–98. "The tunnel of love ... fell all over each other": Rem Koolhaas, *Delirious New York*, pp. 23–29. **Page 142.** *The piers, adjacent to ... and other social outsiders after the 1960s": Richard Renaldi, "The Piers," <www.renaldi.com/ portfolio/pier1.html> (June 18, 2002). "Fire Island, a barrier beach ... mid-twentieth century": Tom Morris, "Fire Island, From Pirates to Slavery to Fun in the Sun," <www.lihistory.com/spectown/ hist0071.htm> (June 18, 2002).

Cracks and Crevices

Page 145. "Here in the home of the Harlem Renaissance ... unashamed mock divas": "Queers in Jazz History" (Queer Jitterbugs), <www. queerjitterbugs.com/jazz_def.html (May 31, 2002). **Page 147.** "... home to never-married women ...'devoted companions' as members": David Bianco, "Before Stonewall Past Out: What Is the History of New York City's Gay Community?, <www.q.co.za/culture/00features/000608- nycgayhistory.htm+Membership+of+ Heterodoxy&rhl=cn&ric-UTF-8> (April 2002). **Page 148.** "In 1646 Jan Creoli ... received a public flogging": E. B. O'Callaghan, ed., *Calendar of Historical Manuscripts in the Office of the Secretary of State, Albany, N.Y.* (Albany: Weed, Parsons, 1865), <www.glinn.com> (May 2002). "Beginning in the early twentieth century ... admitted blacks until the 1960s": George Chauncey, *Gay New York*, pp. 207–25. *Pages 150–51.* "Gays developed extensive ... for daring lesbians": John D'Emilio and Estelle B. Freedman, *Intimate Matters*, pp. 288–95. "Around this time ... or Amy Johns": *The Matrix*, Spring 1999, no. 1, <www.humboldt.edu/ ~hsuwomen/matrix_spr99_1/lesbian%20list. htm> (June 18, 2002). " The erotic energy in bars ... they were better off at home": John D'Emilio and Estelle B. Freedman, *Intimate Matters*, pp. 288–95. **Page 152.** "A certain type of burlesque ... ladies in the audience": *Burlesque in Harlem* (1950, directed by William Alexander, with Dewey "Pigmeat" Markham, Vivian Harris, Jo Jo Adams), <www.somethingweird.com/4090.htm> (June 21, 2002). **Page 154.** "... a time when the meat-

packing plant ... was strictly prohibited": "Greenwich Village: A Gay History" <http:// huzbears.websitenow.com/gayhistory/gv.html> (June 18, 2002).

PART III: THE AVANT GARDE AND SENSATIONALISM

Sex Sells

Page 158. "Sensational, romantic, forbidden ... relatively public view": "Dime Novels, Story Magazines, Pulps," <www.lib.msu.edu/coll/ main/spec_col/nye/dime.htm> (June 1, 2002). "With a new economy ... and *Keyhole* provided it": John D'Emilio and Estelle B. Freedman, *Intimate Matters*, pp. 278–79. **Page 161.** "After the penny press ... masculine-oriented sexual entertainment": Timothy Gilfoyle, *City of Eros*, pp. 99–100, 119, 133–34. "On July 16, 1842, ... not relinquish until finished": George B. Wooldridge, editor and proprietor, *The Whip*, July 16, 1842. "As might be expected ... information on cures for VD": Timothy Gilfoyle, *City of Eros*, pp. 99–100, 119, 133–34. **Page 162.** "At the turn of the twentieth century ... the wise money is on vice": Bradley Smith, *The American Way of Sex*. **Page 164.** "Cigar smoking became a big hit ... winged ladies and Indian maidens": Chip Brooks, "The Need for Labels: The History of Cigar Labels" <www. cigarlabeljunkie.com/html/NeedForLabels.html> (June 11, 2002). **Page 165.** "... the young, smart woman ... smoked, drank and petted": Jessica Forres, "Women's Liberation in the 1920s: Myth or Reality?," <www.gwu.edu/~english/ kaleidoscope/Essaypages/Essay7.htm> (June 18, 2002). "... emerged during World War I ... was the perfect pitch": "Advertising and Consumer Culture," <www.coe.ufl.edu/courses/edtech/ vault/SS/20s/advertisingpage.html> (June 18, 2002). "Women of the era ... their winking days were supposed to be over": Jessica Forres, "Women's Liberation in the 1920s: Myth or Reality? **Page 167.** "Underground erotic publishing ... cause of free speech in jail": Jay A. Gertzman, *Bootleggers and Smuthounds* (Philadelphia: University of Pennsylvania Press, 1999). **Page 168.** "The illegal Tijuana Bible ... famous comic wrapped around bubble gum": Art Spiegelman, introduction, in Bob Adelman, *Tijuana Bibles: Art and Wit in America's Forbidden Funnies, 1930s–1950s* (New York: Simon and Schuster, 1997). **Page 171.** "In *Ginzburg vs. the United States* ... gave prosecutors an edge": "An Overview of Past Pornography Rulings by the Supreme Court," *Frontline*, <www.pbs.org/wgbh/ pages/frontline/shows/porn/prosecuting/ overview.html> (June 21, 2002). **Page 173.** "Al Goldstein launched *Screw* ... life back then in the day": "Slime Marches On:, Celebrating 31 Torrid Years. Screw's Original Credo," <www.screwmag. com/slimeline/slimeline1.htm+Al+Goldstein+ screw+credo&rhl=en&ric=UTF-8> (June 2002).

Page 174. "Two women on the cover ... hotbed of bohemian and gay life": Jaye Zimet, *Strange Sisters: The Art of Lesbian Pulp Fiction, 1949–1969*, with a foreword by Ann Bannon (New York: Viking Studio, 1999). **Page 177.** "Helen Gurley Brown's ... nude male centerfold": www.britannica.com/women/articles/Brown_Helen_Gurley.html> (June 2002). **Page 178.** "In 1922 Ida Rosenthal ... independence in public places": Jennifer Snyder and Mimi Minnick, "Historical Notes on the Maidenform Collection, 1922–1997," Smithsonian American History Archives, August 1997-July 1999. **Page 181.** "Newly returned Vietnam vets ... business boom in New York":James Ridgeway in James Ridgeway and Sylvia Plachy, *Red Light: Inside the Sex Industry*, pp. 216. "The massage is paid for ... available at a higher price": Rebecca Rand, as told to Ridgeway and Plachy in *Red Light: Inside the Sex Industry*, pp. 213–17. **Page 183.** "In the mid-1960s ... battle in the pubic wars": Jack Boulware, *Sex American Style: An Illustrated Romp through the Golden Age of Heterosexuality* (Venice, Calif.: Feral House, 1997), pp. 67–69. Pages 184–85. "Byrd, a fine arts college graduate ... their local cable system": Julian Bain, "Robin Byrd, New York's Best Kept Secret," *Miamigo*, December 2000/January 2001, vol. 3, no. 12. "The most fined man in the history of the Federal Communications Commission": "Howard Stern and His Dysfunctional Radio Family, The First Radio Family," <www.koam.com/hs_radio_fam.html> (June 19, 2002). **Page 187.** "His 1984 men's underwear campaign ... beauty Tom Hinthaus": News editor, "CK Underwear Billboard Causes Traffic Jams," <www.fridae.com/magazine/en20020418_2_1.php> (June 19, 2002).

Bright Lights, Sexy City

Page 189. "... his 1896 film *The Kiss* ... shocked audiences": "Limelight, International Films and the Australian Industry," <www.abc.net.au/limelight/docs/films/5_1_1.htm+Thomas+Edison+the+Kiss&hl=en&ie=UTF-8> (June 23, 2002). "In a 1985 performance ... Josephine Baker": Deepika Bahri, "Grace Jones: 1985 Performance in Paradise Garage," <www.emory.edu/ENGLISH/Bahri/GraceJones.html> (June 23, 2002). **Pages 190–91.** "... an equestrian blood-and-thunder drama ... of the Victorian age": Barbara and Michael Foster, "Adah Isaacs Menken, Broadway's First Star," <www.culturefront.org/culturefront/magazine/2K/summer/article_4.html> (June 19, 2002). "... called 'the naked lady' ... developed woman in the world'": Seymour "Sy" Brody, "Adah Isaacs Menken: Noted Actress and Poet," *Jewish Heroes and Heroines in America, from Colonial Times to 1900: A Judaica Collection Exhibit*, <www.fau.edu/library/brody23.htm> (June 19, 2002). "... a Cossack prince ... galloping to his death": Barbara and Michael Foster, "Adah Isaacs Menken, Broadway's First Star." "In 1866 America's first ... came in handy for both: John Kenrick, "History of the Musical Stage, 1796–1879: Broadway Pioneers," <www.musicals101.com/1860to79.htm> (June 19, 2002). **Page 193.** "On one stretch ... got a thrill": "What Happened on 23rd Street," <www.cs.umd.edu/hcil/ndl/ndldemo/movie2/set1a.html> (June 20, 2001). "Daniel H. Burnham's Flatiron ...'Twenty-three skidoo'": "The Flatiron Building," <www.chryslerbuilding.org/flatiron/flatiron.html> (June 19, 2002). **Page 195.** "Julian Eltinge ... Forty-second Street named after him": Michael F. Moore, "Julian Eltinge Biography," <www.julianeltinge.com/bio.html> (June 20, 2002). **Page 196.** "Isadora Duncan ... a student of the Denishawn Company": Lynne Conner and Susan Gillis-Kruman, "The Solo Dancers: Isadora Duncan, Ruth St. Denis" and "The Modern Dancers: Martha Graham," 1996, <www.pitt.edu/~gillis/dance/isadora.html> (June 20, 2002). **Page 198.** "The dance craze of the 1910s ... Castle Walk, a version of the brisk one-step": "Mixed Pickles' Vintage Dance Timeline: Early 20th Century Dance," <www.mixedpickles.org/20cdance.html+Vernon+and+Irene+Castle+ragtime&hl=en&ie=UTF-8> (June 28, 2002). **Page 199.** "Vaudeville's 'baby vamp' developed her ... convicts and white slaves": "Culture Shock, Theater, Film and Video, Mae West," <www.pbs.org/wgbh/cultureshock/flashpoints/theater/maewest.html> (June 1, 2002). **Page 201.** "Josephine Baker (1906–75) made her mark ... uppity New Yorkers": Lisa Clayton Robinson, "Baker, Josephine," <www.africanaencyclopedia.com/josephine_baker/josephine.html> (June 20, 2002). "Twenty-seven years later ... ovation at Carnegie Hall in 1973": "Josephine Baker Biography," <www.cmgww.com/stars/baker/index.html> (June 20, 2002). **Page 202.** "... outrage and criticism from the press ... vicious hate mail": Kimberly Campanello, *"All God's Chillun Got Wings: Stereotype or Universal Truth?,"* <www.butler.edu/sophist/Secondt.html> (June 22, 2002). "... lawyer-turned-actor": "Paul Robeson: A Brief Biography," <www.cpsr.cs.uchicago.edu/robeson/bio.html> (June 22, 2002). "... a New York Times critic ... very blood of America": John Corbin, *New York Times*, May 18, 1924. "O'Neill, who wrote ...'go fuck yourself'": Kimberly Campanello, *"All God's Chillun Got Wings: Stereotype or Universal Truth?"* **Page 204.** "With her famous ... the dance from time to time": Thomas Gladysz, "Louise Brooks Life and Times," <www.pandorasbox.com/louisebrooks/lifeandtimes.html> and "The Jazz Age: Flapper Culture and Style," www.geocities.com/flapper_culture/> (June 27, 2002). **Page 206.** "The Brooklyn-born Clara Bow ... classic flapper movie": Robert Klepper, "IT: A Review by Robert Klepper" (A Silents Majority Featured Video, 1996), <www.mdle.com/ClassicFilms/FeaturedVideo/video6.htm> (May 25, 2002). "Max Fleischer, the leader of New York–style animation": "Max Fleischer (1883–1940)," <www.zapcartoons.com/bios/max.html+Max+Fleischer+Cartoon+studio&hl=en&ie=UTF-8> (June 27, 2002). "... created Betty Boop ... Miss Boop into boring Betty": Megaera Lorenz, "Betty Boop Before and After the Hays Act," <http://www.heptune.com/boop.html> (June 27, 2002). **Page 209.** "These illegal, titillating, primitive films ... in theaters took their place": Jack Stevenson, "Blue Movie Notes: Ode to an Attic Cinema" (1999), <http://216.239.51.100/search?q=cache:KYGf-jdvWxUC:hjem.get2net.dk/jack_stevenson/blue.htm+stag+film+history&hl=en&ie=UTF-8> (June 29, 2002). **Page 210.** "The Dress—the full-length ... to President John F. Kennedy": "The Most Expensive Gown, Lavish Tastes," Network of the World—India, <http://streaming.now-india.com/convergence/dollar_club/Lavish-Gown.htm> (June 23, 2002). "Adlai Stevenson, who ... goddess's last public performance": "May 19, 1962, Happy Birthday, Mr. President," <www.screenlegends.com/History.htm> (June 23, 2002). "Peter Lawford kept the crowd ... rumors flew": "Happy Birthday, Mr. President," <www.geocities.com/TelevisionCity/Stage/4209/mm/birthday.html> (June 23, 2002). "The star was tentative ... rendition of 'Happy Birthday'": "May 19, 1962, Happy Birthday, Mr. President." "'I can now retire from politics ... sweet, wholesome way'": "Happy Birthday, Mr. President." "In 1999 this perfect ... Christie's for $1.2 million": "The Most Expensive Gown, Lavish Tastes," Network of the World—India. **Page 213.** "Midnight Cowboy (1969) ... generally shocked audiences": Lucia Bozzola, *"Midnight Cowboy,"* <http://www.allmovie.com/cg/avg.dll> (June 2002). **Page 214.** "... along with Kenneth Anger, Gregory Markopolous ... downtown filmmakers":*"Flaming Creatures,"* <www.planetout.com/pno/popcornq/db/getfilm.html?1972> (June 22, 2002). "... abstractions of penises, nipples, feet ... layers of fabric": Anhoni Patel, "Lipstick and Penises: The Origins of Camp. *Flaming Creatures,"* VHS Nation, <www.sfbg.com/AandE/vhs/28.html> (June 22, 2002). "Paying homage to Hollywood ... ecstasy, and general pandemonium": Jack Smith, *"Flaming Creatures,"* <www.hi-beam.net/mkr/js/js-bio.html> (June 22, 2002). **Page 215.** "Drug addicts do anything ... realism in 1970": Chris Barry, "Andy Warhol's *Trash,"* <www.skyhighpictureshow.com/trash.htm> (June 23, 2002). "Holly searches the city's ... baby to get on welfare": "Andy Warhol's *Trash"* (1970) <www.ifilm.com/ifilm/product/film_info/0,3699,2330398,00.html> (June 23, 2002). **Page 216.** "Known as the "Queen of Nudies ... *Each Time I Kill* premiered in 2002)": Luigi Manicottale, "Who Is Doris Wishman?," (2000), <www.doriswishman.com/about.html> (June 23, 2002). **Page 218.** "Who'd have thought ... Joe Davian and Phil Prince": Bill Landis and Michelle Clifford, "The Avon Dynasty: The Avon Theaters of Times Square," <www.geocities.com/moviemags/metasex.html> (June 24, 2002). **Page 219.** *"Deep

Throat (1972) ... forced her to do it": Miss Conduct, *"Deep Throat's* Last Sigh," <www.pigdog.org/auto/bad_people/ link/2555.html> (June 24, 2002). **Page 220.** "Using raw fish, chickens, sausages ... vagina, the source of knowledge": Carolee Shneemann, *"Meatjoy"* (1964), <www.caroleeschneemann. com/works.html> (June 25, 2002). **Page 221.** "When he installed a urinal ... while people walked all over him": Christina Rees, "Art 101: A Conceptual Art Primer," <www.goodbad.org/ press/sidebars.shtml> (June 25, 2002). **Page 223.** "Action painting and happenings ... at 33 Wooster Street": Eleanor Lester, "Is Futz the Wave of the Future?, *New York Times,* June 30, 1968, <www.orlok.com/hair/holding/prepost/ tom/NYT6–30–68.html> (June 15, 2002). "... patron of song, ritual dance, mysticism and winemaking": Alfred Bates, ed. *The Drama: Its History, Literature and Influence on Civilization*, vol. 1 (New York: Historical Publishing, 1906), pp. 215–19, cited in "The Bacchae," <www.imagination.com/moonstruck/ clsc4w1.htm> (June 15, 2002). "Theatergoers could not only ... good feel of their own": Eleanor Lester, "Is Futz the Wave of the Future?" **Page 225.** "'I would either have ended up a nun or this'–Madonna": Jeri Noble, "Celebrity Horoscope: Madonna," www.circlesoflight.com/ horoscopes/madonna.html> (June 15, 2002). "'If I could live my life over again, I'd probably go into the sex industry instead'–Debbie Harry": Biography, Blondie Archive, <www.blondie. ausbone.net/debs.htm> (June 15, 2002). **Page 226.** "The Continental Baths ... in the late 1960s": "The Continental Baths," <www.gaytubs.com/more.htm> (June 25, 2002). "... in the early 1970s ... struggling nightclub singer": "Birth of a Legend, 1970–1974," <www. bettechive.com/betteography/1970_1974 overview.htm> (June 25, 2002). "... on a roster of top entertainers ... went coed and were finally closed": "The Continental Baths." **Page 229.** "When commercial success ... generally entertaining antics": "The New York Dolls," <www.allmusic.com/cg/amg.dll?p=amg&sql= B61967u50h0jd> (June 26, 2002). **Page 230.** "... headed to San Francisco in the 1970s ... go into skeevy theaters": "Live Chat with Candida Royalle," <www.planetrapido.com/carnal/ sexperts/candida/candida1.htm> (June 25, 2002). "A founding member of the New York– based ... comes to sex on screen": FFE board of directors, Candida Royalle, <www.ffeusa.org/ board/royalle.html> (June 25, 2002). **Page 233.** "... at the Second Coming, a New York conference ... performance center, Franklin Furnace": Maria Elena Buszek, "Of Varga Girls and Riot Grrrls: The Varga Girl and WWII in the Pin-up's Feminist History," <www.ku.edu/~sma/vargas/buszek. htm+Carnival+Knowledge+Franklin+Furnace&hl= en&ie=UTF-8> (June 28, 2002). "... Franklin Furnace in trouble with the NEA": "Franklin

Furnace in Time," <www.franklinfurnace.org/ timeline/timeline.html+Carnival+Knowledge+ Sprinkle&hl=en&ie=UTF-8> (June 28, 2002). **Page 234.** "Throughout his career ... socio- political issues": Richard Covington, "On, Dancer," *Salon,* March 28, 1997, <www.salon.com/ march97/jones2970328.html> (June 26, 2002). "... from upstate New York ... and love in 1971": Julinda Lewis-Ferguson, "Free to Dance Biographies: Bill T. Jones," <www.pbs.org/wnet/ freetodance/biographies/jones.html> (June 26, 2002). "... collaborating with artists and designers ... and Willi Smith": Lisa Phillips, *The American Century: Art and Culture, 1950–2000* (New York: Whitney Museum of American Art, in association with W.W. Norton, 1999), pp. 345–46. "... pre- miered Still/Here ... Brooklyn Academy of Music": "Bill T. Jones/Arnie Zane, The Company," <www.geocities.com/Broadway/Balcony/3252/ company.html> (June 26, 2002). "Arlene Croce of the *New Yorker* ... and (sexual) politics": Lisa Phillips, *The American Century: Art and Culture, 1950–2000.* "In the late 1990s ... focus solely on movement": Richard Covington "On, Dancer." **Page 237.** "The breakthrough film for the Brooklyn-based ... want her for their own": *"She's Gotta Have It* Film Info," <www.ifilm.com/ifilm/ product/film_info/0,3699,2327370,00.html> (June 26, 2002). "... winner of the Prix de Jeunesse ... independent film movement of the 1980s": "Spike Lee Biography and Jointography" <www.inmotionmagazine.com/slee2.html> (June 26, 2002). **Page 238.** "Karen Black, the star ... rock band named after her": Frank Reardon, "The Voluptuous Horror of Karen Black," <www.horror-wood.com/black.htm> (June 26, 2002). "Combining burlesque, vaudeville ... lead's vagina and is typical ...": "The Voluptuous Horror of Karen Black," <www.allmusic.com/cg/amg.dll? p=amg&sql=B26ri288r05ja> (June 26, 2002). "A photograph in *The Anti-Naturalists* ... vagina sewed shut": Ted Watts, "Voluptuous Horror Isn't Scary," <www.pub.umich.edu/daily/1995/ 10–395/arts/Voluptuous.html+The+Voluptuous+ Horror+of+Karen+Black&hl=en&ie=UTF-8> (June 26, 2002). **Page 240.** "... star of more than 150 porn films ... activist and performance artist": "Doctor G's Erotica Reviews," <www.doctorg. com/erotica_reviews.htm> (June 16, 2002). "Knowing no taboos ... deviousness are universal traits": Theresa Stern, interview with Lydia Lunch (October 1997), <www.furious.com/perfect/ lydialunch.html> (June 18, 2002). **Page 243.** "But Lil' Kim, from Bedford Stuyvesant ... M.A.F.I.A. group ...": "Lil' Kim Biography," <www.mtv. com/bands/az/lil_kim/bio.jhtml> (June 26, 2002). *Hard Core* (1996) ... *Billboard* Top 200": "Lil' Kim" <www.rollingstone.com/artists/ default.asp?oid=2956> (June 26, 2002).

Culture Shocking

Page 244. "... Christ's last supper that features ... 'outrageous and disgusting'": "Naked Jesus

Angers Giuliani," *BBC News,* February 16, 2001, <http://news.bbc.co.uk/hi/english/world/ americas/newsid_1172000/1172837.stm> (June 2, 2002). "The use of color sets ...'the perfect antidote for excess conventionalism'": <www. baroness.com/index.htm> (June 2, 2002). **Page 247.** "Nudes, especially by Old Masters ... set by the prudish middle class": John D'Emilio and Estelle B. Freedman, *Intimate Matters,* pp. 157–58. "Critics condemned the painting ... of sexual intercourse": William H. Gerdts, *The Great American Nude: A History in Art* (New York: Praeger, 1974), pp. 39–41. "... special days were set aside ... nude figures with delight'": John D'Emilio and Estelle B. Freedman, *Intimate Matters*, pp. 157–58. **Page 249.** "... (the powerful thirteen-foot-high statue ... eighteen-foot version was out of proportion)": letter from Sigmund Rothschild to Ralph Miller, June 5, 1968, courtesy Museum of the City of New York. "Victorian moralists had a problem with ... now at the Philadelphia Museum of Art": Lloyd Morris, *Incredible New York,* pp. 165–66. **Page 250.** "The model for Paul Chabas's *September Morn* ... its postcards remain big sellers": Bonnie Bull, "The September Morn Story," <www.bullworks.net/ ffg/sptmrn/sptmrn.htm> (June 27, 2002). **Page 253.** "Salvador Dali, the European ... scales on a human piano": Rem Koolhaas, *Delirious New York,* pp. 223–28, *Life,* March 17, 1939. **Page 255.** *Femme Maison* (housewife)": David Cateforis, associate professor of art history, University of Kansas, "Louise Bourgeois," <http:// 216.239.51.100/search?q=cache:di6XwFQYOyQC: old.jccc.net/main/docs/news_entertainment/ cec/gallery/htms/Bourgeois.htm+Louise+ Bourgeois,+Femme+Maison&hl=en&ie=UTF-8> (June 27, 2002). "Vriesendorp painted a postcoital scene ... humorless RCA Building": Alexandra Lange, "White Out: New York Times Unveils Plan to Create New Eighth Avenue Home; Piano Design Hailed as Breakthrough for Manhattan Skyline," *New York Times,* February 4, 2002, <www.metropolismag.com/ html/content_ 0402/nyt/+madelon+vriesendorp&hl=en&ie= UTF-8> (June 27, 2002). **Page 256.** "Bettie Page was probably ... on camera or in print again": "Bettie Page: A Short Biography," <www. sexualtimes.com/gallery/bpage/bio/bpbio.html> (June 27, 2002). **Page 258.** "Henry Miller's (1891–1980) *Tropic of Cancer* ... were described in detail": Bradley Smith, *The American Way of Sex,* pp. 225–26. "The characters in this tale of ribald sexual exploits": Wendy Moss, "Henry Miller, 1891–1980," <www.levity.com/corduroy/ millerh.htm> (June 14, 2002). "... proud of their sexuality and their sexual organs": Bradley Smith, *The American Way of Sex,* pp. 225–26. "... sold two million copies in two years": Wendy Moss, "Henry Miller, 1891–1980." "... GI's smuggled it into the States ... it was unpublishable": Bradley Smith, *The American Way of Sex,* pp. 225–26. "Barney Rossett of Grove Press ... the status of fine art":

"DWIM, Henry Miller," <www. litkicks.com/ BeatPages/page.jsp?what=HenryMiller>(June 14, 2002). **Page 261.** "... most 1950s comedians did strings of jokes and stories": Steve Allen on Lenny Bruce, <http://216.239.35.100/search?q=cache: 8D_v7NBcQgwC:members.aol.com/dcspohr/ lenny/allen.htm+Lenny+Bruce+comedians+before &rhl=en&ie=UTF-8> (June 29, 2002). "... he was arrested for obscenity four times ... Café au Go Go in Greenwich Village": Peter Keepnews, "There Was Thought in His Rage," *New York Times,* August 8, 1999, <www.duckprods.com/projects/ lb/lbnytimesfeature.html+Lenny+Bruce+trial+ New+York&rhl=en&ie=UTF-8&re=619> (June 29, 2002). "Bruce wondered why ... 'sick comic' and a 'dirty comic'": Ralph J. Gleason, "An Obituary," <http://members.aol.com/dcspohr/lenny/ obgleas.htm> (June 29, 2002). "Bruce finally got a career-ending ... alleged herion overdose": Peter Keepnews,"There Was Thought in His Rage."
Page 263. "Liberating masturbation ... *The Joy of Selfloving*": "About Betty Dodson," <www. bettydodson.com/betbio1.htm> (June 28, 2002).
Page 264. "Brooke Shields took her first ... a twelve-year-old prostitute": "Brooke Shields Biography: A Class Celebe," <www.aclasscelebs. com/brookes/biocontact.htm+Brooke+Shields+ photo+Garry+Gross&rhl=en&ie=UTF-8 (June 27, 2002). "One of his images ... his name added to any exhibition labels": Nina Teicholz, "Hard Copy: It's Tough to Tell who Gets the Credit for a Notorious Picture of Brooke Shields," <www. newyorkmag.com/page.cfm%3Fpageid%3D1695 +Brooke+Shields+photo+Garry+Gross&rhl=en&ie =UTF-8> (June 27, 2002). **Page 265.** "A self-described hick ... Karen Finley, and other": "Biography," <www.richardkern.com> (June 28, 2002). **Page 267.** "... native Long Islander": "Biography" (The Mapplethorpe Foundation, Inc.), <www.mapplethorpe.org/biography.html> (June 14, 2002). "... had his first big shows ... at the Kitchen": "Robert Mapplethorpe Biography," <www.guggenheimcollection.org/site/artist_bio_ 97A.htm> (June 14, 2002). "Senator Jesse Helms . . . crotch showing, around with him as evidence": Margaret Quigley, "The Mapplethorpe Censorship Controversy: Chronology of Events," The 1989– 1991 Battles (Political Research Associates), <www.publiceye.org/theocrat/Mapplethorpe_ Chrono.htm> (June 14, 2002). **Page 268.** "... on the rise in the 1960s ... obvious canvas for their nicknames": Ayana Walker, "History of Grafitti," <www.albany.edu/~aw2882/history.html> (June 26, 2002). **Page 269.** "For folks who want . .. costume designer for television and film": "Patricia Field, Costume Designer, *Sex and the City,* HBO," <www.hbo.com/city/cmp/insiders_guide/ cast_and_crew_field.shtml> (June 28, 2002).
Page 271. "In the late 1980s ... Duchamp-inspired R. Mutt Press": John Held Jr., "Pictures That Kill," in *Badlands: Photographs of Charles Gatewood*, (Frankfurt: Goliath Press, 1999), pp. 20–24.

Public Displays

Page 272. "Although New York has a state law ... essentially unenforceable": Organizers of New York City's Lesbian, Gay, Bisexual and Transgender Pride March, Rally, Dance and Pridefest, "Heritage of Pride," <www.nycpride.org> (June 6, 2002). **Page 275.** "... estimated fifty thousand ... Party in New York": "Women Don't Want It: Where Were the Suffragists?" *The Woman's Protest,* June 1912, p. 7, <http://216.239.35.100/search?q= cache:Gtcq7ZGJTYsC:1912.history.ohiostate.edu/ suffrage/amendment.htm+Suffragists+1912+New+ York+City&rhl=en&ie=UTF-8> (June 28, 2002). "... lobbied, used civil disobedience ... vote in national elections": "The Featured Document: The 19th Amendment," <www.nara.gov/exhall/ charters/constitution/19th/19th.html+Suffragist s+1912+New+York+City&rhl=en&ie=UTF-8> (June 28, 2002). "For New York's first large ... to show their resolve": "Woman's Suffrage and Abolition Movement Timeline, 1910–1919," <www.coax.net/people/lwf/1910_19.htm+ Suffragists+1912+New+York+City&rhl=en&ie= UTF-8> (June 28, 2002). "Not everyone was pleased ... questioned the attendance figures": "Women Don't Want It: Where Were the Suffragists?" **Page 276.** "On her way up ... on to successful professional careers": Kathryn Leigh Scott, *The Bunny Years* (Los Angeles: Pomegranate Press, 1998). **Page 278.** "After midnight on June 27, 1969, ... Sheridan Square in Greenwich Village": "Stonewall Rebellion" (The Knitting Circle: History) <www.sbu.ac.uk/stafflag/ stonewall.html> (June 28, 2002). "Although they had been paid off ... charge of serving alcohol": Leslie Feinberg interview with Sylvia Rivera, "I'm Glad I Was in the Stonewall Riot" (Workers World News Service, reprinted from *Workers World,* July 2, 1998), <www.workers.org/ww/1998/ sylvia0702.html> (June 28, 2002). "Sympathetic crowds gathered ... throwing bottles": "Stonewall Rebellion." "Molotov cocktail": Leslie Feinberg, Leslie Feinberg interview with Sylvia Rivera, "I'm Glad I Was in the Stonewall Riot." "Violent protests challenging ... last Sunday of June": "Stonewall Rebellion." **Page 279.** "Angry women took to the streets ... keep women in fear": Aaron Greenwood, "Collected Quotes from Feminist Man-Haters (collection by starbuck@galaxy.ucr. edu), <www.vix.com/men/bash/quotes.html> (June 28, 2002). **Page 282.** "Drag Queens, porn stores ... Chicago Underground Film Festival": Camille Paglia, June 2002. **Page 283.** "However, in June 2001 the *New York Post* ... St. Regis Hotel suite as a love nest": "N.Y. Mayor in 'Love Nest' Row," CBSNews.com, via MMI Viacom Internet Services Inc., <www.cbsnews.com/stories/2001/ 06/06/politics/main295140.shtml> (June 28, 2002). **Page 285.** "... two thousand-person ... rebellion a year earlier": "Pride History" (The Knitting Circle), <www.sbu.ac.uk/stafflag/ pridehistory.html> (June 6, 2002). "... attracts 250,000 marchers ... millions of dollars to the city": Organizers of New York City's Lesbian, Gay, Bisexual and Transgender Pride March, Rally, Dance and Pridefest, "Heritage of Pride," <www.nycpride.org,> (June 6, 2002). "Since 1992, on the Saturday beforehand ... to combat discrimination": "10th Annual New York City Dyke March—A Decade of Dykes ... Doin' 'til We're Satisfied!, <www.lesbiannyc.com/ dykemarch> (June 6, 2002).

Scenes

Page 288. "Count Basie, a Savoy regular ... and triggering fights": Austin Graham, "Hip, Hot and Headbanging: The Retro Rebirth of Swing," <http://216.239.51.100/search?q=cache:04rn 8AAQb0AC:xroads.virginia.edu/~CLASS/am483_ 97/projects/graham/movement.html+Jitter bugging+at+the+savoy&rhl=en&ie=UTF-8> (June 29, 2002). "Jitterbug (originally meaning those who loved to swing dance)": "Dance Terms and Dates, Jitterbug," <www2.kenyon.edu/ Depts/IPHS/Projects/swing1/dance/terms.htm+ Jitterbugging+at+the+savoy&rhl=en&ie=UTF-8> (June 29, 2002). "... coined by the trombonist-arranger ... Benny Goodman": "Jitterbug," <www.streetswing.com/histmain/z3jtrbg.htm> (June 29, 2002). **Page 290.** "Sex was central to Andy Warhol's ... beautiful bohemian girls": *Andy Warhol* (American Masters), <www.pbs.org/ wnet/americanmasters/database/warhol_a. html> (June 2, 2002). "Nude Restaurant, starring ... primarily wearing G-strings": Gary Comenas, *The Nude Restaurant* (Warhol Stars, 1967), <www.warholstars.org/warhol/warhol1/ warhol1f/restaurant.html> (June 2, 2002). **Page 292.** "Studio 54 at 254 West Fifty-fourth ... get past the doorman": Kelly Wittmann, "Studio 54 History," <http://216.239.51.100/ search?q=cache:wx44z8do1rYC:or.essortment. com/studiohistor_raxp.htm+Studio+54+history& hl=en&ie=UTF-8> (June 29, 2002). **Page 295.** "It's uncertain ... reached 50,000 in 1995 at the piers": "History of Wigstock" (2001), <www. wigstock. nu/history/history.html> (June 2002). "A Fiorucci boutique regular ... his idol, Billie Holiday": Joey Arias, "Queen Mother, Free the Queen Within," <www.queenmother.tv/nycgirl/ joey/joey.html> (June 2002). **Page 297.** "The Jackie 60's Archives," <www.mothernyc. com/jackie/60.html> (June 2002). **Page 301.** "... the Swiss-born, London-inspired ... vogueing dance trend in the early 1990s": Louis Canales, "Vive La Bartsch!,," *Miamigo*, vol. 3, no. 12, December 2000/January 2000). **Page 302.** "Heterosexual women ... must be accompanied by women": "Club.Cake," <www.cakenyc.com> (June 16, 2002).

Anything Goes

Page 305. "... endless array of sexual possibili-ties": Introduction, *Sexy New York City 2001: The Annual Guide to NYC Erotica.* "Doris Kloster, an accomplished photographer ... powerful, real-life sex radicals": Doris Kloster, *Forms of Desire* (New York: St. Martin's Press, 1998. <www.stonewallinn. com/Features/FormsIntro.html> (June 8, 2002).

Page 307. "... dildos, cock rings, lubricants ... typically women in their twenties": Robert T. Michael, John H. Gagnon, Edward O. Laumann, and Gina Bari Kolata, *Sex in America: A Definitive Survey* (New York: Warner Books, 1995), cited in *Carnal Knowledge Face Off: Sex Toys*, Knotmag.com (April 11, 2002), <www.knotmag.com/%3F column%3D11+sex+toy+shops+New+York+City& hl=en&ie=UTF-8&e=619> (July 1, 2002). "... ongoing focus on sexually explicit material": Greg Sargent, "Bloomberg Grapples with Eleventh Hour Giuliani Sex Dicta, *New York Observer*, July 1, 2002, <www.observer.com/pages/story.asp% 3FID%3D5409+Giuliani+adult+video++restriction s&hl=en&ie=UTF-8> (July 1, 2002). **Page 308.** "Not until Frank Pernice and Larry Levinson ... America's number one sex club": Sean Rowe, "Swingers Redux," <www.newtimesbpb.com/ issues/1998-06-11/news_toc.html> (June 16, 2002). **Page 310.** "Manhattan's biggest sex venue ... Show World at Times Square": Wayne Hoffman, "Mickey and the Peep Show," *The Nation*, October 18, 1999, <http://216.239. 51.100/search?q=cache:JmPwhCMYWZAC:past. thenation.com/issue/991018/1018hoffman. shtml+show+world+peep+New+York+city&ie= en&start=10&ie=UTF-8&e=747> (July 1, 2002). "Here a love team ... four-tokens-for-a-dollar-deal": Guy Gonzales, July 1, 2002. "...'crossroads of the World' ... keeping its video booths":

Wayne Hoffman, "Mickey and the Peep Show." **Page 313.** "With so many high-powered execs ... latex-clad, whip-wielding tough cookie": Christopher Mele, "City's X-rated Businesses Blue Over Decline," *The Journal News*, November 12, 2001, www.thejournalnews.com/shocks/ as_111201.html+New+York+Dominatrixes&hl= en&ie=UTF-8> (July 1, 2002). **Page 314.** "Til Eulenspiegel, who enjoys ... frowns when striding down": Theodore Reik, "Masochism in Modern Man" (excerpt), The Eulenspiegel Society, <www.tes.org/about/faq.html> (June 30, 2002). "Founded informally by masochists for masochists ... requirement of a truly free society'": The Eulenspiegel Society, <www.tes.org/welcome. html> (June 30, 2002). **Page 316.** "Rena Mason, a horror-movie costumer ... mistress did in her own good time": James Ridgeway and Sylvia Plachy, *Red Light: Inside the Sex Industry*, pp. 95–104. **Page 319.** "A group of guys ... Albolene and paper towels": Peter Palmer and New York Jacks, <www.nyjacks.com/jxindex.html> (July 1, 2002). **Page 319.** "... the Hellfire, New York's original BDSM ... insertables must be covered in latex": Hellfire Club information, <www. hellfireclubny.com/homepage.htm> (July 1, 2002). **Page 320.** "Other notorious drag kings are Labio ... Dréd and Lizeracé": "The Drag Kings of Club Casanova," <www.pipeline.com/ %7Ejordinyc/kings.htm> (July 1, 2002). "Murray Hill, known for ... Rudolph Giuliani in 1997": "Murray Hill," <www.mrmurrayhill.com> (July 1, 2002). "Mo B. Dick launched Club Casanova ...

with socks or dildos": *New York Post*, June 23, 1996, and Press-Club Casanova Online, www.pipeline.com/%7Ejordinyc/ccnews01/ index.htm> (July 1, 2002). **Page 322.** "... the nation was full of anxiety ... Operations Transform Bronx Youth (*New York Post*): Susan Stryker, "Christine Jorgensen," <www.planetout. com/news/history/archive/jorgensen.html+ cHRISTINE+jORGENSEN&hl=en&ie=UTF-8> (June 30, 2002). "Dr. Hamburger performed ... as charismatic Christine": Marlene Peters, "The Christine Jorgensen Memorial Gallery," <www.geocities.com/marlenepeters_2000/ christine.html+cHRISTINE+jORGENSEN&hl= en&ie=UTF-8> (June 30, 2002). "Christine wanted to live quietly ... lucrative nightclub business": Donald P. Myers, "A Changed Man: Long Island, Our History," <www.lihistory.com/ 8/hptjorg.htm+cHRISTINE+jORGENSEN&hl= en&ie=UTF-8> (June 30, 2002). "... in 1993 by Veronica Vera, a writer ... Vera's clients are straight": George Rush, *New York*, February 8, 1993, <http://www.missvera.com/press/nymag/ nymag.html> (June 30, 2002). **Page 324.** "Male-to-female trannie stars ... out of the most amazing places": Nora Burns, "Red Lights, Big City," *Time Out New York*, no. 266, October 26–November 2, 2000), <www.timeoutny.com/ features/266/266.ft.sex.shows.html> (June 17, 2002). "When they lost their dancing jobs ... their careers and reputations": "Dancing Queens, Clubbers," April 19, 2001, <www.clubbed.com/ clubbers/article1092.asp> (June 16, 2002).

© **Barbara Alper:** Page 317 (*Fetish Factor Party*, 1992). Page 319 (*Spanking Spectacle, Hellfire Club*, 1981). © **Merry Alpern·** Page 118 (From *Dirty Windows*, no. 5, 1994. Courtesy Bonni Benrubi Gallery, NYC). **American Antiquarian Society:** Page 18 (*Cries of New York*, 1818). Page 36 (*Aristotle's Compleat Masterpiece*, 1755). Page 37 (*A Sentimental Journey through France and Italy*, 1795). Page 49 (*Catherine Sedgewick*). Page 51 (*A Scene from the Laughable Comedy of the Divorce Suit*, ca. 1860s). Pages 52–53 (*The Seven Stages of Matrimony*, Nathaniel Currier, ca. 1860s). Page 95 (*The Three Graces*, James Baillie, 1848). Page 124 (*A Grand Ball with Julia Brown, Flash*, 1843). Pages 160–61 (*The Weekly Rake*, July 9, 1842). Pages 190–91 (*Mazeppa*, 1846). **The American Way of Sex: An Informal History,** by Bradley Smith (New York: Two Continents, 1978): Page 64 (*The Oneida Commune, National Police Gazette*). © **AP/Wide World Photos:** Page 75 (May 10, 1999). Page 81 (May 13, 1968). Page 200 (1936). © **Arrow Productions:** Page 219 (*Deep Throat*, with Linda Lovelace, 1972). © **Les Barany:** Page 241 (*Annie Sprinkle at the Kitchen*. Courtesy Annie Sprinkle). © **Bettmann/CORBIS:** Page 92 (1850s daguerreotype). Page 114 (Seaman First Class Murray Berlin gets a big kiss from the Chinese "Pinup Queen," Noel Toy, at the Latin Quarter to celebrate the end of World War II, August 15, 1945. Shirley Stevenson, Lorraine Rogers, and Evelyn Lewis wait their turn). Page 127 (*Brothel*, Reginald Marsh, 1928. Photograph © Geoffrey Clements). Page 132 (August 28, 1985. © Ezio Petersen). Page 154 (October 26, 1962). Page 187 (*Times Square*, 1982). Page 199 (*Sex*, with Mae West, February 10, 1927). Page 211 (May 19, 1962). Page 322 (April 1956. © Sam Schulman). © **Brooklyn Museum:** Pages 108–9 (*The Haymarket*, John Sloan, 1907). **Brown University Library:** Page 59: ("*Horrors upon horrors accumulate. Discovering the body at the depot. The curtain lifted on the tragedy.*") Page 70: (*The Beecher and Tilton War*). **Robin Byrd Show:** Pages 184–85. © **Vincent Cianni:** Page 318 (*New York Jacks*, 1988. Courtesy Vance Martin Photography and Fine Art, San Francisco). © **Martha Cooper:** Page 268 (*Airborne*, 1981). © **Cosmopolitan Magazine, Inc.:** Page 176 (Paula Pritchett, *Cosmopolitan*, November 1967. Photograph by Francesco Scavullo). Page 177 top (Sandra Hilton, *Cosmopolitan*, May 1966. Photograph by Francesco Scavullo; bottom (Paula Pritchett, *Cosmopolitan*, November 1966. Photograph by William Connors). **Creative Time:** Pages 280–81 (*Kissing Doesn't Kill*, 1989–90. Bus poster campaign by Gran Fury. A Creative Time Project). © **Daily News L.P.:** Page 74 (August 26, 1986). Page 184 (Book party at the Harley Davidson Cafe, October 1993. © Richard Corkery). Page 186

(April 2000. © Richard Corkery). Page 283 (December 31, 2001. Photograph by Craig Warga). © **Delaware Art Museum:** Pages 44–45 (*Man, Wife, and Child*, John Sloan, 1905). **Delirious New York: A Retroactive Manifesto for Manhattan,** by Rem Koolhaas (New York: Oxford University Press, 1978, p. 84): Page 107. **Dell Publishing Company, Inc.:** Page 131 (*The Happy Hooker*, Xaviera Hollander, 1972). © **Betty Dodson:** Pages 262–63 (Drawings from *Liberating Masturbation: A Meditation on Self Love*, 1974). © **Johnny Dynell:** Page 297 (June 1992). **Erotica Universalis,** by Gilles Neret (Cologne: Taschen, 1994): Page 28. © **Donna Ferrato:** Pages 292–93 (*Studio 54*, 1979). Pages 308–9 (*Plato's Retreat*, 1981). Pages 314–15 (*Eulenspiegel Society*, 1980). © **Leonard Fink, Courtesy National Gay and Lesbian Archives:** Pages 88–89. Page 307. © **Forty Acres and a Mule Filmworks:** Pages 236–37 (*She's Gotta Have It*, by Spike Lee, 1986). © **Paul Fusco/Magnum Photos:** Pages 156–57 (*Parades and Changes*, Anna Halprin Dance Company, 1965). © **Andrew Garn:** Page 135 (*Silver on the Deuce*, 1986). Page 310 (*Show World Stage*, 1984). © **Charles Gatewood:** Page 270 (*Spider Webb Opening at Levitan Gallery*, 1976). Page 287 (*Nude Man Painted Gold*, 1975). Pages 312 and 313 (*Emily at her Loft*, 1995). **Gemäldegalerie Alte Meister, Staatliche Kunstsammlungen Dresden:** Page 17 (*The Procuress*, Jan Vermeer, 1656). **Jay Gertzman Collection:** Page 166 (*Sacred Prostitution and Marriage by Capture*, G. S. Wake. New York: Big Dollar Book Company, 1932). Page 167 (*Criminal Identification Files*, Philadelphia, June 1930). © **Edwin Gifford with Lisa Fiel:** Page 295 (*Joey Arias at the Roxy*, 1994). © **Barbara Gladstone:** Page 221 (*Seedbed*, Vito Acconci, January 15–29, 1972. Performance and installation at Sonnabend Gallery, NYC). **Thomas Gladysz, The Louise Brooks Society:** Page 204 (attributed to Alfred Cheney Johnston, 1920s). Page 205 (*Blue Nude*, George White Studio, 1925). © **Efrain John Gonzalez:** Pages 320–21 (*There He Blows! Hey Mo!*, 1994). © **Garry Gross:** Page 264 (*Brooke in Tub*, 1975). © **Fred Gurner:** Page 130 (*Xaviera's Bedroom*, 1971). Page 131 (*Xaviera Reclining*, 1971). **Leo Hershkowitz Collection, Courtesy American Antiquarian Society:** Pages 12–13 (1850). Page 39 (1808). Page 57. Pages 66–67 (1840). Page 97. Page 123 (1839). **The Historical Atlas of New York City,** by Eric Homberger (New York: Henry Holt, 1994, p. 87): Page 42 (*Mose and Lize*). **History of Contraception Museum, Janssen-Ortho Inc.:** Pages 78–79. © **Hollywood's Attic 1996:** Pages 152–53 (*Burlesque in Harlem*, 1949). © **Ray Hörsch, www.eroto.com:** Cover (*High Rise*, 1996). Page 2 (*New York Flasher*, 1995). **Incredible**

New York: High Life and Low Life from 1850 to 1950, by Lloyd Morris (Syracuse: Syracuse University Press, 1951, p. 87): Page 48 (*New York Herald*). **John D. Kahlbetzer Collection:** Page 254 (*Femme Maison*, Louise Bourgeois, 1946–47. Courtesy Cheim & Read, NYC. Photograph by Rafael Lobato). © **Richard Kern:** Page 265 (*Monica in the Elevator*, 1993). © **Doris Kloster:** Page 304 (*Tami*, 1997). © **Bettye Lane:** Page 218 (*Porn Movie Strip*, 1971). Page 279 (*Women Against Porn Demonstration*, 1979). **Leather Archives and Museum:** Pages 154–55 (*Men at the Mineshaft*, ca. 1976–85). **Lesbian Herstory Archives:** Page 175 (*21 Gay Street*. Midwood, 1962. Cover art by Paul Radar). **Library of Congress, George Grantham Bain Collection:** Page 274 (Fay Hubbard, 1910). **Library of Congress, Prints and Photographs Division:** Page 22 (*The Inconvenience of Wearing Coffee Bag Skirts*, James Baillie, 1848). Page 56 (*The Weaker Sex II*, Charles Dana Gibson, *Collier's Weekly*, July 4, 1903). Page 72 (Arnold Genthe, ca. 1913. Arnold Genthe Collection). Page 76 (ca. 1910). Page 80: (H. C. Miner Litho Company, New York, 1918–20). Page 198 (© 1913 by Moffett). **Library of Congress, Rare Book and Special Collections Division:** Page 162 (1905). Page 163 (ca. 1900–1910). **Library of Congress, TV Reading Room and Motion Picture Reference:** Page 192 (*What Happened on 23rd Street*, Thomas Alva Edison, 1901). **Alison Maddox Collection:** Page 21 (*Little Known Facts About Bundling in the New World*, Monroe Aurand Jr. Aurand Press, 1938). Page 82: (1906). Page 91. Pages 104–5 (H. C. Miner Litho Company, New York, ca. 1888). Page 113 (Alberto Vargas, 1930s). Page 116 (1950). Page 158 (*He*, 1953). Page 159 (*Confidential*, 1950s). Page 256 (attributed to Irving Klaw, 1950s). © **Copyright by the Estate of Robert Mapplethorpe:** Page 266 (*Untitled*, 1981. Used with permission). © **Vivienne Maricevic:** Pages 310–11 (*Live Sex Shows, 711 Theatre*, 1983). © **2002 Estate of Reginald Marsh/Art Students League, New York/Artists Rights Society (ARS):** Pages 140–41 (*New York Spooks—The Tunnel of Love*, Reginald Marsh, 1943). © **Ben Martin:** Page 260 (*Lenny Bruce Leaving Courthouse*, 1966). Page 264 (*Steinem at Shakespeare Ball*, 1964). © **Misa Martin:** Page 336 (*Domina Britt-Liberty*, 1998). **Vance Martin Photography and Fine Art, San Francisco:** Pages 84 and 85 (Edwin F. Townsend, 1930s and 1932. Private collection). © **Mashala:** Page 269 (*Sexy–American Pride*. A benefit for the September 11th Fund hosted by Patricia Field, NoHo, fall 2001). Pages 324–25 (*The Magic Show*, Amanda Lepore and Sophia Lamar. A tribute to the legendary international Chrysis and benefit for Breast Cancer Research, Slipper Room, NYC, spring 2000). **Massachusetts Institute of**

Technology, Lewis Music Library: Page 110 (anon., 1919). © Dona Ann McAdams: Pages 232–33 (Carnival Knowledge, 1983). Page 233 (Penny Arcade, 1985). Page 235 (Continuous Replay, P. S. 122, 1991). © Fred W. McDarrah: Page 278 (Stonewall Inn, June 29, 1969). © Mark McQueen: Page 245 (The Baroness–Bizarre Garden Party, 2000). © 1983 Metropolitian Museum of Art: Pages 250–51 (September Morn, Paul Chabas, 1912. Purchase, Mr. and Mrs. William Coxe Wright Gift, 1957, no. 57.89). MGM Clip+Still: Page 212 (Midnight Cowboy. © 1969 Jerome Hellman Productions, Inc. All rights reserved). F. Michael Moore: Page 194 (The Crinoline Girl, 1914). Page 195 both (Cousin Lucy, 1915). © Paul Morrissey: Page 215 (Trash, with Joe Dallesandro and Holly Woodlawn, 1970). © Muna Tseng Dance Projects, Inc., NYC: Page 188 (Photograph by Tseng Kwong Chi, 1985). © Museum of the City of New York, www.mcny.com: Pages 32–33 (Baroness von Riedesel Treated Courteously by General Schuyler, 1777). Page 34 (from Footnotes exhibition. Gift of Mrs. Randolph Jenks). Page 63 (The Man-Monster, Peter Sewally, alias Mary Jones, 1836). Pages 120–21 (Hooking a Victim, Serrell and Perkins, 1850). Page 164 (1903). Page 248. Musicals101.com: Page 191 (The Black Crook, 1866). © Billy Name: Pages 290–91 (Andy Warhol Directs Taylor Meade and Viva in Nude Restaurant, 1967. Courtesy Ovoworks, Inc.). © National Museum of Fine Arts, Stockholm: Pages 246–47 (Danae och Guildregnet, Adolph Ulrich Wertmuller, 1787). © Marco Nero: Page 231 top (Blue Magic, with Candida Royalle, 1980). © Collection of the New-York Historical Society: Page 19 (New Year's Day in Old New York, G. H. Boughton, Peters Collection, no. 49875). Page 24 (Dancing Scene Outside a Dutch Tavern, no. 24415). Page 26 (Unidentified Woman, Formerly Edward Hyde, Lord [Viscount] Cornbury). Pages 40–41 (Five Points, Intersection of Cross, Anthony, and Orange Streets, 1827, Valentine's Manual of Old New York, 1885, p. 112, no. 44668). Page 47 (The Close of the Winter Campaign, Harper's Weekly, May 5, 1877, no. 75257). Pages 54–55 (Sulpher Bitters ad, Landauer Scrapbook 22, no. 75265). Pages 60–61 (The Innocent Boy, lithograph by A. Hoffy, ca. 1836, no. 40696). Page 68 (Anthony Comstock, Pach photograph, no. 49875). Page 69 (Be Saved by Free Love, Thomas Nast, Harper's Weekly, February 17, 1872, p. 140). Page 106 (no. 75263). Pages 128–29 (Frank Leslie's Illustrated Newspaper, May 12, 1883, Harry Peters Collection). Page 149 (Everard's Turkish Baths, 28 West Twenty-eighth Street, no. 56229). New York Public Library, Astor, Lenox and Tilden Foundations, General Research Division: Page 35 (Fanciful Images of Maria Reynolds and Her Lover, from Alexander Hamilton, American, by Richard Brookhiser. New York: Free Press, 1999). Page 100–101 bottom (Recollections of a New York Chief of Police, George W. Walling, 1887, p. 493). Page 122 (The Madam, from The Women of New York, or,

Social Life in the Great City, George Ellington, 1869, p. 198). Page 125 (Canal Street Cigar Store Visited by a Tract Distributor, from The Women of New York, or, Social Life in the Great City, George Ellington, 1869, p. 172). Page 126 (Queen of the Underworld, from The Women of New York, or, Social Life in the Great City, George Ellington, 1869, p. 244). Page 138 (Fast Women in Central Park, from The Women of New York, or, Social Life in the Great City, George Ellington, 1869, p. 238). Page 165 (The Cosmopolitan, Rochester, N.Y., May 1923, p. 164). New York Public Library, Astor, Lenox and Tilden Foundations, Milstein Division of U.S. History, Local History and Genealogy Division: Page 14 (pen-and-ink sketch of native woman and fish, Jaspar Danckaerts, Journal of a Voyage to New York, 1679–80). Page 100–101 top (Sunshine and Shadow in New York, Matthew H. Smith, 1868, p. 434). Page 102 (Valentine's Manual of Old New York, vol. 12, 1928). New York Public Library, Astor, Lenox and Tilden Foundations, Miriam and Ira D. Wallach Division of Art, Prints and Photographs: Page 16 (engraving, Nieu Amsterdam, 1642–43, I. N. Phelps Stokes Collection, Deak no. 32). Page 20 (Old Times on Broadway, M. Osborne, Emmett Collection, no. 10514). Page 25 (color lithograph, The Battery: New York by Moonlight. Nathaniel Currier, 1850. Eno Collection, no. 272). New York Public Library, Astor, Lenox and Tilden Foundations, Schomburg Center for Research in Black Culture, Photographs and Prints Division: Pages 150–51 (Portrait of Two Young Men on Couch, 1950s. Photograph by Glenn Carrington. Glenn Carrington Collection). Pages 288–89 (Jitterbugging at the Savoy Nightclub, ca. 1939). New York Public Library for the Performing Arts, Astor, Lenox and Tilden Foundations: Page 196 (attributed to Arnold Genthe, 1916. Jerome Robbins Dance Division). Page 197 (White Studio, NYC, 1920s. Jerome Robbins Dance Division). Page 203 (All God's Chillun' Got Wings, with Paul Robeson and Mary Blair, 1924. Billy Rose Theatre Collection). © Barbara Nitke: Page 231 bottom (Candida Royalle directing Revelation, 1992). Page 273 (All Slaved Out, 1997). © Tina Paul, fifibear.com: Pages 238–39 (The Voluptuous Horror of Karen Black at CBGB's 25th Anniversary, 1993). Pages 284–85 (Gay Pride Parade, 1992). Page 294 (Wigstock at Pier 54, 2001). Page 300 (Susanne Bartsch Prom Night Party, Chelsea Piers, 1994). Page 301 (Party for Liz Torres at Downtown, 1989). © Penthouse Magazine: Page 182 (Avril Lund, Pet of the Month, Penthouse, March 1973. Photograph by Bob Guccione). Page 183 (first U.S. edition of Penthouse, September 1969). © Sylvia Plachy: Page 86 (Dr. Brad Jacobs, Manhattan). Page 298 (Clit Club). Page 316 (Ms. Rena and Client, Manhattan). © Plaster Foundation, Inc: Page 214 (Flaming Creatures, Jack Smith, 1963. Courtesy Anthology Film Archives). © 1980 Playboy: Page 277 (Photograph by Frank Eck). Pleasure Chest NYC: Page 306.

George Rinhart Collection: Page 99 (1880s). Mark Lee Rotenberg Collection, www.vintagenudephotos.com: Page 83 (1920s–30s). Page 136 (1940s). Pages 168 and 169 (She Ate a Hot Dog at the Word's Fair, 1939). Page 170 (Eros, summer 1962). Pages 180–81 (1973). Pages 208–9 (Gigolette, 1931). Page 256 top (Camera Club photograph, ca. 1955). Page 257 top (ca. 1955); bottom (plastic surgeon's slide case used as nudie frame, 1950s). © Rob Roth: Page 296 (Click and Drag, 2001). James E. Routh Jr. Collection: Pages 30–31 (Stephen Tambling Horn, 1761, 5½" long, attributed to Richardson Minor, Lake George School, Crown Point, N.Y. Courtesy Connecticut Historical Society). © Carolee Schneemann and PPOW, NYC: Page 220 (Meatjoy–Kinetic Theater, Carolee Schneemann, 1964). © Martin Schreiber: Page 225 (Madonna, 1979). © Jenny Schulder: Pages 302–3 (Courtesy Cake, L.L.C., cakenyc.com). © Screw Magazine: Page 172 (Screw Comix, no. 4, 1996). © Tony SetteDucate: Page 143 (Morning Party, Fire Island Pines, 1997). Bradley Smith Archives: Pages 258–59 (Henry Miller, Pacific Palisades, 1971. © Bradley Smith). Smithsonian Institution, National Museum of American History, Archives Center: Page 179 (Maidenform Collection, 1962). Smithsonian Institution, National Museum of American History, Medical Sciences: Page 79. South Hampton Partners, Ltd: Page 207 (Be Human, with Betty Boop, 1936. Original art by Max Fleisher). © Annie Sprinkle: Page 240 (Lydia Lunch, 1990s). Star File: Page 117 (© Dominick Conde). Page 224 (© Chuck Pulin). Pages 228–29 (© Bob Gruen). Page 242 (© Todd Kaplan). Staten Island Historical Society, Staten Island, N.Y. 10306: Pages 146–47 (ca. 1905). © Tracy Tippet: Page 282 (Glennda and Camille Do Downtown, directed by Glenn Belverio, 1993). Jan Van Der Donk Rare Books, Inc.: Pages 252–53 (Dream of Venus installation, Salvador Dali, 1939. Photograph © Eric Schaal). © Donna Mussenden VanDerZee: Page 144 (Beau of the Ball, 1927. Photograph by James VanDerZee). © Pierre Venant/Women's Wear Daily: Pages 226–27 (February 4, 1972). © Veronica Vera: Page 323 (Miss Vera's Finishing School for Boys Who Want to Be Girls, by Veronica Vera. New York: Doubleday, 1997). © Madelon Vriesendorp: Page 255 (Flagrant Delit, 1975, from Delirious New York: A Retroactive Manifesto for Manhattan, by Rem Koolhaas. New York: Oxford University Press, 1978). © Max Waldman Archives: Page 222: (Dionysus in 69, 1969. Photograph by Max Waldman). © Ting Li Wang/New York Times: Page 133. © Weegee/ICP/Getty Images: Page 150. © Meike Williams: Page 299 (Cyber Sluts, 1995. Courtesy Mother, NYC). © Doris Wishman: Page 216 (Bad Girls Go to Hell, with Gigi Darlene, 1965). Page 217 (Deadly Weapons, with Chesty Morgan, 1973). © Worldview Entertainment: Pages 206–7 (It, with Clara Bow, 1926).